HIGH
VOLTAGE

HIGH VOLTAGE

A.B. GIBSON

STORY MERCHANT BOOKS
LOS ANGELES • 2018

High Voltage

ISBN: 978-1-7323411-8-0

Story Merchant Books
400 S. Burnside Avenue, #11B
Los Angeles, CA 90036
www.storymerchantbooks.com

To Julieann

Acknowledgments

Thank you to Brianna Maguire, my trusted editor and co-conspirator in many projects.

Prologue

The sudden clatter was loud enough to scare a dead man from his grave.

"Jesus! Who's there?"

The lack of a visible moon made the night nearly pitch black in the vegetable garden. It was only after emerging from the shadows and stepping into the faint glow from a low-wattage floodlight fifty yards away that the identity of the stumblebum who knocked over the metal wheelbarrow was revealed.

"Oh, you startled me. I didn't expect anyone else up."

"Digging's cooler at night."

"Makes sense. I wish I thought of that when I was digging."

"Looks like you're all packed to go somewhere."

"Yeah, I decided to leave. Tonight."

"I thought you told me you were staying."

"I was. My friend and I both were, but I guess he left."

"Yeah, people come and go around here."

"Maybe, but it's strange he left without telling me."

"Well, he must have."

"Yeah, I guess."

"So, what are you doing out here in the garden?"

"I wanted to see the place one more time before I left."

"Oh."

"Well, I gotta get going."

"Okay. Don't let me keep you. Be safe."

The hiker walked a few yards into the dark and stopped. "Listen, something really weird is going on around here and I think I know who's behind it. Want to know my theory?"

Whap! The edge of the spade cracked the hiker's skull just above the ear.

"No."

PART ONE

1

When I posted on social media that I had a couple weeks to kill, I didn't mean it literally.

I was being transferred to our office somewhere in southwestern Pennsylvania and wouldn't have to report to work for another month, so I decided to burn off some vacation time. Over coffee one morning, an older colleague mentioned my transfer and pointed out how lucky I would be to live near the Appalachian Trail, which he called one of the wonders of the world. It surprised me when he said he once hiked the whole two thousand miles, and the picture he painted sounded both beautiful and challenging. He claimed the experience changed his life.

"It can change yours, too," he said. "You don't need to hike the whole enchilada. Give yourself a week or two and start with a small section to see how you like it."

Going hiking and camping by myself was nothing I ever thought to do, but the idea intrigued me. I told him I'd only camped once before and didn't own a stick of equipment. And when I confessed that—because I'd be shelling out a lot of money for my move—I wasn't in a position to invest in any, he snickered, and I soon understood why.

He offered to give me his old gear. His hiking days had been over for a long time, and he was tired of the flak his wife gave him for all the space the stuff took up in their basement. He said I'd be doing him a big favor by taking it off his hands. He planned to donate it to a thrift shop, anyway. I'd have what I'd need to get started—backpack, tent, cook set, everything. I could hardly turn him down.

I'd only been camping once with my next-door neighbor's family as a kid and, while I don't recall many details, I remembered having a blast. Camping as an adult would be a different experience and I had no idea whether I'd like it, but the offer was fortuitous. The move would put a dent in my checkbook, so a fancy vacation was out of the question. How could I lose?

"There is one more thing you'll need, though—something I can't give you. You'll need a trail name," he added.

A trail name was a nickname in the hiking world. Everyone on the Appalachian Trail went by one. The names typically related to hiking or nature or the outdoors, but lots of hikers took ones that played to a personal characteristic. My colleague wore a size fourteen boot, so people called him Big Foot.

"Spend a few minutes and pick one you like. You'll keep it for the rest of your life."

I needed no time at all because I already had the perfect one, a nickname someone gave me when I ran cross-country in high school. Nobody had called me that for a long time, but I always liked the name and it would be fun to resurrect. It sounded confident, sleek, and elegant. I'm not sure which motivated me more, the exciting prospect of hiking the Appalachian Trail or the fun of a re-branding. But, I was so charged, I updated my social media profiles and started posting online using my new old identity: *Strider.*

Along with his gear, my colleague passed on a couple of guidebooks, and the more I read, the more fired up I got. One guide came with a map that made planning my first two-week hike to Harpers Ferry and back super easy.

Like a lot of thirty-five-year-old single guys, I didn't own much in the way of furniture, so it was easy to pack everything in a U-Haul and dump it in the apartment I'd rented a few weeks before. I knew no one in my new location, so I'd have plenty of free time in the evenings for a while, and I intended to unpack and set things up when I got back from my Appalachian Trail adventure. Besides, I wanted to spend as much time hiking as I could.

Since I was an avid runner and still had plenty of stamina, I knew the hiking part would be a snap. As a camper, though, I was a complete novice and I blew it on day one. The fresh air exhilarated me, and I got so caught up in the experience I lost track of the time. I failed to notice the rain clouds gathering, too, and I got caught in a heavy downpour.

I had already passed one campsite, and by the time I got to the next, I was drenched. So was my sleeping bag because I'd made the mistake of hanging it on the outside of my pack without its protective cover. Fortunately, there was a sleeping space left in the campsite shelter so at least I didn't have to deal with pitching my tent in the rain and the dark.

I was glad I was smart enough to pack several snacks and sandwiches to get me by for the first couple of days so I didn't have to tackle cooking that first night. Unfortunately, I was stupid and forgot to bring bug spray, so mosquitos and other mysterious insects feasted on me all night.

My luck changed when I woke to a beautiful seventy-degree day. Remarkably, my things had dried overnight, and I had the chance to start over. I was so focused on my pace and ticking off mileage posts to stay on the timetable I'd created, that I didn't pay enough attention to the magnificent views and abundant wildlife the trail had provided.

I thought about the online quiz I took that determined I didn't enjoy living in the moment. At the time, I rejected its conclusions, but the test ended up being right, and the proof was staring me in the face. I wasn't good at living in the present. But it wasn't my fault. I just didn't know how. Until trail magic intervened and I met Daisy.

The trail had twisted sharply to the right and exposed a spectacular lookout even I couldn't miss. I climbed on a large inviting boulder where I drank in sweeping vistas for miles in three directions. Believing I was the only one there, I stretched out my arms and shouted to the sky, "This is f-f-freaking amazing!"

Crap! That stutter never left me in peace. Happy no one was around to hear me, I repeated it louder, just to enjoy the extra reverberation from the mountains.

"It sure is," came a female voice in a mock echo from behind me.

I jumped and spun around to see an adorable woman, about fifteen years younger, with dark, wavy hair and big doe eyes standing on the path below. I was so taken off guard, I lost my balance and skidded down the boulder.

As I began to teeter off the edge, the woman grabbed my hand to steady me before I fell and made a complete fool of myself. And, even though I landed on my feet and the stumble was awkward, I was more embarrassed she witnessed my stutter.

To compensate for my lame dismount, I spoke in a strong, deep voice. "I'm actually pretty c-c-coordinated."

She gave me the once-over. "I'll bet you are," she said, slinging on her backpack. "Which way are you headed?"

I got so flustered by her interest that I had to look in both directions. Then I grinned and pointed. "That way."

"Me, too," she said. "My name is Daisy, short for Daisy Duck. Mind if I hike with you for a while? I promise to keep up."

I was stunned.

Daisy walked next to me rather than in single file, which sent nervous jitters down my spine. She probably felt it would make it easier to converse, but, due to my stutter, conversation with strangers was something I always dreaded. That fear led me to a career in computer programming, an occupation where I could be socially isolated. But, Daisy seemed unfazed by my stupid stutter. In fact, she told me later that she found it sexy.

We both enjoyed the fresh air and the physical rigor of climbing each rise in the trail, and her company was exhilarating. And, she'd pull me over from time to time look at a flower or piece of tree bark, some natural phenomenon I would never have observed on my own. And, sometimes, she would stop me simply to listen.

"What kind of bird is that?" I asked the first time.

"I have no idea. And don't ask me the names of these trees or flowers either, because I won't know them."

I laughed. "And here I thought I was hiking with an expert."

"No, but everything is so beautiful, don't you think? Here's what I mean," she said, pointing up into the trees. The sky was bright and the sun was blinding. "It's kind of like Photoshop. The sunlight paints all these amazing colors and uses leaves as the filters."

I started to pay more attention to the beauty around me and, before long, perceived the journey becoming more interesting than the destination. This Daisy, who had dropped out of the sky, was showing me a whole new way of looking at the world, and hiking alongside her that afternoon turned my worldview upside down. When I pointed out what was happening, she dismissed my compliment with a laugh.

We pitched our tents next to each other, and she delighted me by offering to share her food, but she put me on the spot when she asked me to build the fire. This would be my first one built from scratch, and I was terrified to fail. She pretended to be busy preparing dinner, but I could see her glance over occasionally as I struggled.

"I'm good at a lot of things," I said after my first few attempts resulted in smoldering failures. "But I guess you can tell I suck at this, huh? If you've got any great ideas, please feel free to speak up. I'm not macho about stuff like this."

"I'm not that good at starting fires, either. Why do you suppose I asked you? Perhaps if we tried using smaller sticks. I'll go find some."

I was relieved that she didn't care that I made a fool of myself. Later, when she embarrassed herself by burning the pasta, I realized why.

"I have an idea," she said. "Since we're both sort of new at this, why don't we hike together a little longer while we learn the ropes? What do you think?"

A little while turned into two very agreeable days of long hikes, breathtaking views, and crackling campfires. Daisy made the ideal companion in my new co-adventure, and I marveled that each day a new skill replaced a bit of my camping ineptitude. Even building a fire and cooking for two became a comfortable routine, and I gave all the credit to her.

I wondered how I deserved such happiness with a girl who wasn't turned off by my handicap or my incompetence. Maybe there was such a thing as love at first sight. I felt like the male lead in a rom-com who'd met the girl of his dreams. I only hoped my feelings weren't the result of my recent rebound from a difficult online relationship.

It was a quiet, starry night at the end of a glorious day together, and Daisy and I were enjoying the twinkling lights of Harpers Ferry from our perch on a log bench at the Maryland Heights scenic overlook.

She broke the silence. "Penny for your thoughts?"

I could feel her dark, brown eyes staring at me, but a serious case of the jitters kept me from returning her gaze. Instead, we both kept staring at the soft moon.

"I was thinking about how much I've enjoyed these few days." I swallowed hard. "I think we make great p-p-partners."

I wanted to seduce her by delivering a great line, but I didn't know how, and I fell flat. I didn't think my stuttering helped either, and, when she didn't respond, I felt stupid for what had come out of my mouth. I immediately took another stab at it and only made things worse.

"I mean, we've both gotten so c-c-competent, and we work so well together."

She laughed. "Is that your idea of a pickup line?"

I was nervous and not sure if she was making fun of me or not, but I took heart that she at least picked up on the intention behind my idiocy.

We sat in uncomfortable silence for a while, and since she said nothing further on the subject, I took it as disinterest. I'd never had much luck with women and I lost confidence again, until I felt her take my hand. She held me tight, and my heart started to race.

And that's when Daisy spilled the beans. "It's good you're sitting down. I have a confession to make."

"Huh?" I braced myself for the bubble that was about to burst.

"I haven't been truthful." Her delivery was as dramatic as the panorama. "I'm a fraud."

It was a punch to my chest. I wanted to get up and run away from her and the whole insane idea that she might be the one to complete me. But something made me stay. I shifted around uncomfortably on the log and tried to pull my hand away. She resisted and instead gave it a little squeeze.

I was confused and eager for her to get to the point. "What do you mean, a fraud?"

She took her time. "I knew the names of all those flowers and trees back there."

"What?"

"And remember that first dinner I cooked for you?"

"How could I forget? It took me all night to start the f-f-fire."

"I burned it on purpose."

"Huh? Why?"

"Actually, I've been doing this since I was a kid. Not the lying part, but, you know, the hiking and camping thing."

"Is that all?" I was relieved. "Well, you sure fooled me."

At last, she looked into my eyes. "And that was the point. When we met, you said you'd never camped before and didn't understand what you were doing. As we both know, you proved that over and over. But I liked you the minute I saw that cute butt of yours standing up there on that boulder. And when you turned out to be a good guy, too, I played dumb, thinking I'd trick you into hiking with me."

I inched in. "Got any other tricks up your sleeve?"

"Maybe."

Then we were in each other's arms.

• • •

When we emerged from her sleeping bag late the following day, she caught me off guard by saying she was interested in a commitment. Later, when the trail led us into the charming town we'd seen from the lookout the night before, she dropped hints about moving in together. I was crazy about her, but things were happening a little fast for me.

Harpers Ferry is a hiker's mecca and the halfway point in the over two-thousand-mile Appalachian Trail. There are ruins to explore and museums to visit, and we spent the day ducking in and out of one charming shop after another. It was near closing time when, in a dusty secondhand store with a cute name, Daisy asked the clerk to show her something locked in a display case.

"Wow, Strider! Can you see the little leaves and vines carved all around the sides? It would make the perfect engagement ring."

My heart did a little dance. "A wh-wh-what?"

She waved away my surprise. "Or, you know, a promise ring. Just something symbolic."

"But you said engagement. Do you really think you want to marry me?"

Her eyes skittered over to the clerk who pretended not to listen. "Well, not *right now* but I hope eventually we can. I mean, we love each other, don't we?"

Married? Love? The mere thought left me speechless. While I barely knew her, I couldn't deny that as I watched her fondle the ring and gaze up at me with such hopeful eyes, my heart skipped a beat.

I didn't know what to say, and the longer I stayed silent, the more rejection I saw in her face, and I couldn't bear to see her disappointed. Besides, calling it a promise ring didn't sound as serious.

"Go ahead, try it on," I said, regretting the suggestion.

The clerk gave the ring a quick polish. "Well, look at that," he said, admiring the splendid fit. "It was made for you."

Daisy threw her arms around me. "Oh, Strider, can we buy it, please? I'd be the happiest woman in the world."

I hugged her back, but I couldn't muffle my nervous laugh. "Er, how m-m-much?"

Buying an inexpensive trinket was something I could always rationalize, but when the clerk said two hundred dollars, my face fell.

The euphoria of the previous twenty-four hours blurred everything. Since Daisy turned my libido upside down, hiking became an afterthought, and the Appalachian Trail merely a setting for our nonstop sex. I questioned whether I was thinking with my brain.

Two hundred dollars was out of the question, and I was sorry she didn't realize it. Our conversations had been reduced to the silly kinds of gibberish that often accompany a new fling. We certainly didn't speak about our finances.

I realized how entirely unprepared I was for this escalating relationship. I brought her to the corner of the store, where I confided in private that as much as I'd like to buy it for her, I was strapped for cash. To make my move across the country, I'd temporarily maxed out my credit cards, and I was down to my last few bucks.

"We'll have to think about it," I told the clerk. It was heartbreaking to watch her remove the ring, and, as she handed it back, I made her a promise to find a way to buy it.

He overheard me and, eager to make the sale, he pulled out a card. "Here. This farm is popular with hikers looking to pick up some quick cash. To make it easy, they encourage you to camp right on their property. You may want to give it a try."

I thanked him for the referral, but we still left the shop disappointed. Determined to turn our mood around, I suggested we at least celebrate our commitment with dinner at a real restaurant.

Daisy pitched in a crumpled ten-dollar bill she found in her pocket but, even after pooling the rest of our resources, we only had enough for cheeseburgers and fries at The

Tankard, a bistro down the block someone had recommended. I wanted to toast being officially broke by splitting a beer.

"You can drink it all. I'm starving and need solid food," she said. "So, as long as this is all the money we have, I'd rather have another order of fries."

When a restaurant is packed, you know the food is going to be good, and the fries were world class. We couldn't keep our hands off each other and, though we were surrounded by strangers, we enjoyed flirting, to show off we were a couple.

I'm not sure when I started to get the strange vibe that someone was watching us. I scanned the room twice, but nothing struck me as out of the ordinary.

Some local guys were shooting pool, and a crowd two-deep were keeping the bartender busy, and, even though logically I could tell nothing was wrong, I couldn't shake the feeling that something was off. I wanted to leave. But Daisy was ravenous, and we stuck around long enough for her to finish everything on both our plates.

We woke up the next morning penniless and determined to find some temporary work. The server at the restaurant gave high marks to the farm we mentioned, but somehow farm work didn't sound substantial enough, and we had something more traditional in mind.

Finding such a job turned out to be impossible, but not for lack of trying. We went up one side of the main street and down the other, and no one was interested in hiring two hikers on a short-term basis. That was when I reached into my pocket for that card.

"Shoot," I muttered. "We m-m-must have left it at that bar last night."

When we returned to the Lost and Found to get another one, the clerk was thrilled to see us and asked if we had come back to buy the ring.

I was embarrassed. "Actually, that's why we're here. I'm afraid we're still a little sh-sh-short and wondered if you could give us another one of those cards you gave us yesterday? We'd like to work at that farm for a couple of days, after all."

"Of course." He nodded. "But I can help you even more. Give me a moment."

He disappeared into the back room, and, by his muffled voice, I could tell he was making a phone call. When he came back out, he was smiling.

"I inquired with the farm's owner, and she says there's space for two more hikers. I told her you were interested and that you might head her way. Here's another one. I wrote the directions on the back."

I couldn't imagine how I missed it before, but as I held the hand-written card, the generous offer burst into view. *Day Workers Needed. $100 a day. Winter's Farm.* A hundred dollars a day was huge, and I did some quick calculations. If we both worked a week, we'd be sitting pretty. In two weeks, we'd be rich, at least by hiker standards, and it would be a simple matter to slip out, come back, and buy her the ring.

Daisy and I agreed to give the farm a try. If all went well, we'd stay as long as we could stand the work and earn as much money as possible. In spite of our disappointing experience in the store the day before, we figured fate brought us there, and we were very lucky, indeed.

2

The directions on the back of the card took us along a narrow, unimproved, and poorly marked country road. We had to double back at least once because we made a wrong turn, and even accounting for some quickie sex in an abandoned pig pen, getting to the farm took longer than we expected.

The Winter's Farm sign that greeted us was desperately in need of paint, but it directed our eyes to a long driveway leading past a farmhouse to a cluster of barns and a picnic table, with a sign that read *Hikers' table*. We barely took our seats before a vintage sedan drove up.

The glare from the sun on the windshield blocked our vision at first, but soon we saw the tip of an unusual cane drop to the ground from behind the driver's door, and a woman hobbled around to greet us. Silver hair was piled on her head, hastily pulled back with a clip that wasn't quite doing its job. She complemented her faded and oversized housedress with mud-stained hiker boots and a string of pop beads. She had a kind face and small but sturdy body aside from the one mangled leg.

I was so amazed by her grand entrance, that Daisy poked me and said I was staring.

"Look at that view!" the woman boasted, sweeping her cane across the horizon. "I never get tired of it. My full name is Ethel Marie Winter, Missus, but call me Ma, everyone does. Since Pa died a few years back, this little arrangement with hikers has helped me keep my farm. My farm needs workers, and you need cash. I call that a win-win."

She pointed to the campsite behind one of the barns. "You can pitch your tents over there anywhere you like. When you're done, come back, and I'll show you what to do." There was a slight twinkle in her eye. "And the shower is next to the latrine. I'll bet you could use them both."

Judging by the number of tents set up in the campground, other hikers were at work. We were only using one tent now, and, because in our new physical relationship we could get a little boisterous at night, we thought the others would benefit if we camped as far away as possible. After taking long showers, we reported for duty.

Since I took up with Daisy, I thought my physique was getting soft, and I was eager for some serious manual labor. Ma didn't disappoint me when she assigned me to work on the raised beds in the large vegetable garden. Some needed weeding, others cultivating, and more had to be dug and built from scratch. I eagerly grabbed a spade and joined another hiker who was already working.

Daisy's job was not nearly as strenuous. She and another female hiker were assigned to help Ma in the kitchen putting up produce. Daisy worried that her inexperience would be a problem because she hadn't canned anything before, but Ma set her at ease and promised to make both women experts. As proof of her credentials, she pointed to the wall of blue ribbons she earned over the years.

Back in our tent later that night after our first half-day of work, Daisy kept me in stitches with a hysterical blow-by-blow account of her adventures in the kitchen. I laughed my butt off as she flawlessly imitated Ma's voice and mannerisms.

"'The. Two. Most. Important. Things.' Ma punctuated each word with a finger jab in the air. 'To understand about canning are that ingredients got to be fresh, and everything's got to be sterile.'"

Putting up produce historically allowed the family to get through the rest of the year and was serious business at Winter's Farm. Canning also contributed to the farm's revenue, because anything they didn't consume themselves, she was allowed to sell to the public, or so said the certificate, which asserted that she met the standards of the local Health Department.

"'If you're not scrupulous, bad things can find their ways into them jars, and we don't want to get into trouble with botulism. Now, which one of you wants to be my "chop-chop" girl?' Ma made a point of turning the left side of her head toward them. 'Be sure to speak in my good ear, now. I'm deaf in the other one.'

"On the floor next to the long butcher block table was a row of bushel baskets filled to their tops with vegetables. She wiped off a large knife on her apron and handed it to the other girl, instructing her to start with the beets.

"'Make 'em so big,' she said, using her thumb and index finger to show the exact size.

"The other girl was a real pro," Daisy recounted. "She cut the beets into perfect pieces like she had done it a thousand times before."

Daisy's job was to wash about two hundred dirty and dusty canning jars and lids that had been stored in some collapsed old cardboard boxes on the floor in a corner.

"Can you believe I asked her what the jars were for? I was confused because she told us we were canning. Talk about clueless."

Even I knew people use jars for canning, and I couldn't resist a snicker.

When the beets were cut up, Daisy said Ma clapped her hands and told them to switch jobs. The other girl didn't mind reporting to the sink, but when Ma brought up a basket of carrots to chop, Daisy was terrified.

"Strider, Ma watched my every move. You should have seen her. She scared the daylights out of me."

While she was studying her new sous-chef struggling to cut up the carrots, Ma got caught in a loud sneeze. She blew her nose on a crumpled hanky that she pulled out of her bosom. Then, she stuffed it back in. When she felt watery mucus on her fingers, she retrieved the damp hanky again, passing it from hand to hand until she wiped all the mucus off.

"'Land sakes!' she exclaimed, her eyes watering. 'Only one thing makes me sneeze like that—ragweed! But how could any end up in my kitchen?'

"I hope you don't mean these?" Daisy said she asked her, holding up a few flowering stems. "I found them growing around the campsite. I thought they were pretty, and I was hoping you could identify them for me.

"Ma didn't waste a moment. She scooped up the offending weed with a dishtowel and rushed me out of the house, instructing me to toss them on the burn pile at the other side of the backyard. She was still sneezing when I returned.

"I was hoping she'd at least wash her hands after all that, but, instead, she grabbed a handful of carrots I was cutting up and examined them one by one. When she saw that I wasn't chopping the way she liked, she totally lost it. 'No, no, no,' Ma barked, dropping her soggy handkerchief on the butcher block. 'You're doing everything all wrong. Let me show you.'

"Under her direction, the blade moved at the speed of light, and, within seconds, she had my first batch of carrots sliced on the bias and into strips. She grabbed another bunch and began anew, but she was only halfway through when she sneezed again, and this time her knife nicked her knuckle.

"'Land Sakes!' she yelped again. For a tiny little cut, it bled profusely. She grabbed at her snotty hanky again and managed to get blood all over it and her housedress. Finally, she stuck the wounded finger in her mouth.

"By then, Ma's snot and blood were on everything," Daisy laughed. "And I wondered when the sterilization part she talked about was going to begin."

Ma seemed less concerned about sanitation and more troubled about Daisy's lack of skill it appeared. Daisy said she told the other girl to take over with the vegetables and asked her if her handwriting was better than her chopping. Daisy was relieved to be assigned to a job she didn't suck at.

"Ma pointed vaguely at an old chest of drawers and told me to get some markers and labels. I was nervously rummaging through one drawer, when the girl at the sink spoke up. 'I'll get them.'

"She dried her hands and pulled open a drawer I had previously examined, and she found everything. The labels had a little sketch of the farmhouse, and Ma pointed to the blank space at the top. 'Write Brody's Beets on this one and Chloe's Carrots on the other, and make the names big now, so I can read 'em when they're setting up on the shelf and I'm down here.'

"From floor to ceiling, an entire wall of wooden shelving held over two hundred canning jars, meticulously grouped by vegetable. Most of them were dusty on the outside, but the brilliant colors were still visible through the glass. All bore identical labels and were identified by personal names.

"'We like to remember the hikers that helped grow the vegetables, so we put their names on the jars. Each time I open one it's like going down memory lane. Like them beets. They're real good, but dang if that Brody wasn't a lazy little guy.'

"'Can I get something named after me?' I asked. She said we both could. I was mesmerized by the variety: peas, beans, cauliflower, and—oh my God! 'Are those hooves?' I asked her. I couldn't believe it.

"'Penny's Pigs Feet,' Ma replied proudly. 'Best in the county. Wait here. I'll fetch you some seeds and you can pick out what you want.'

"From behind one of the jars, she retrieved a key to a room off the kitchen. She re-emerged with a box. 'Here they are. You can plant 'em in the garden for posterity.'

"'You keep seeds locked up?' asked the other girl.

"'Got to. They're precious. They go way back, and we don't want to waste 'em.'"

Daisy told me what she chose.

"Thought *dill* had a nice ring to it," she said. "Besides, it was the only seed that started with 'D.' The other girl picked radicchio, I think."

"Wow, compared to yours, my day was boring," I said. "I basically dug ditches with another guy, and we didn't say more than two words to each other."

For the next two days, I continued to dig, and I didn't mind that the work was boring, because I was happy to build back my upper-body strength. Besides, Daisy's job was exciting enough for us both, and she kept me laughing every night with tales of Ma's kookiness.

The following morning, Ma declared it was payday, and we all reported to the kitchen where, with a bit of fanfare, she doled out cash to everyone. She gave us a wink as she passed us our stacks of tens, and, when we counted our money, we were thrilled to receive an unexpected bonus.

She paid us a hundred dollars each for that first day, even though we'd only worked a half day. Three hundred dollars each was a fortune, and we spent the night having sex under the worn-out, ten-dollar bills we spread out like Monopoly money over our sleeping bag.

Sometime in the night, I got up to use the bathroom and found another hiker sitting by a small campfire. For a second, I almost mistook her for a man. Her hair was cropped short, and her clothes were loose fitting, not unusual for trail dwellers. I remembered that her hiker name was Tornado, and I was almost sure she'd been planting pumpkins with an Australian hiker. She smiled and waved me over.

"Nice kicks," I said, gesturing to her PF Flyers.

"Thanks. Having a good night?" she asked mischievously as I plopped down beside her. Her comment made me blush. In spite of the distance between our tent and the rest of the hikers, Daisy and I hadn't exactly been quiet.

"Yeah, you c-c-could say that."

"Are you guys serious?"

I scratched my head, not quite sure how to answer. Daisy certainly was. She seemed to think we were on the verge of getting engaged. But I was not accustomed to taking risks, especially when my love life was at stake.

"Sort of," I replied. "We've only known each other a short time, but she already wants to get m-m-married."

I expected a judgment from Tornado that never came.

"Cool," she said. "You guys would make a cute little family."

"You don't think jumping into marriage is a bit nuts?"

Tornado raised an eyebrow. "Do you? Love is about taking risks, right? Seems like the sort of thing people who are crazy for each other always do."

What Tornado said made sense on paper but reality had a way of mucking things up. Getting married or even seriously involved with someone I'd only known for a few days was too wild for me despite it being unquestionably romantic.

Then again, being careful hadn't helped either. I'd been burned so many times I couldn't honestly say that I was ever this close to getting married. And I had never been this attracted to someone before. Maybe the idea wasn't so crazy after all.

"How old are you, by the way?" Tornado teased. "Shouldn't you be married with grandkids or something?"

I rolled my eyes. "I'm thirty-five not sixty."

Tornado put her hands up in defense. "Hey, I'm just saying, clock's a'tickin.'"

I always thought the idea that a person needed to be married or have kids by a certain age was baloney, but I confess to having those same thoughts recently. I'd checked all the boxes on the way to starting a family: I was mature, I had a nice new job, and I'd even rented an apartment with two bedrooms.

I shook my head. "True, but Daisy's only twenty or so, and I doubt she's thinking of marriage that way."

Tornado rapped her knuckles gently against my head. "Are you hollow in here? Wasn't it *her* idea to get married in the first place?"

"Sure, I guess."

So, I decided to take the plunge and buy the ring. I had already made enough cash, and there could be plenty more where that came from. But to make sure the ring would be a surprise, the next morning I made up a story about how Ma asked me to go to town for some supplies.

I told Daisy the errands would take the better part of the day, and that I would be back in time for dinner. She made the decision easy for me by offering to stay at the farm to work, so our income stream would be uninterrupted.

It would be a long walk down and back and I would have to hustle, so I left all my stuff in our tent and took only my money and a water bottle. As I was walking down the driveway, Ma intercepted me and insisted I join her on the front porch for a cup of coffee. I got a later start than I expected. I wanted to be polite, but she jabbered on and on and I felt awkward leaving.

The trip took longer than I remembered, too, and by the time I arrived, the shop was about to close. The clerk, who turned out to be the owner, recognized me through the window and was more than willing to stay open to make the sale. He told me my timing couldn't be better, because, while the ring had not yet sold, I wasn't the only one to have it under consideration. He unlocked the case and held Daisy's ring up to the light.

"You know, I'd be happier if you'd let me clean it for you. I'll only be a few minutes."

I agreed and followed him to the jeweler's bench where he examined it under a large magnifying glass. Almost immediately, he shook his head.

"Oh, no. I'm sorry. I can't sell you this."

My heart sank. Daisy would be so disappointed to hear our precious ring had a defect. And after all that effort. "Why not?"

"If you squint, you can make out the tiny inscription on the inside, 'Dillon and Pat.' Other people's names won't do on a new couple's engagement ring and would certainly bring bad luck. Let us buff out their names and engrave the ring properly with your own. I'd be happy to throw in the service for free, as our little gift."

Decisions, decisions. I didn't want Daisy to worry about me, but it was too late for that. I was already going to miss dinner, and no doubt she'd found out that I'd lied about running errands from Ma by now.

But the ring was engraved with other people's names. I hadn't heard of that superstition before, but I hated the idea that something so preventable might bring us bad luck. And the engraving would be the perfect touch. I took him up on his offer and thanked him profusely, hoping I'd made the right decision.

There was only one hitch. The owner had an appointment in a few minutes, but he promised to take care of my engraving first thing in the morning. He was very sorry, and he hoped the slight delay wouldn't be a problem.

While I would have to stay over in Harpers Ferry and Daisy would be alone for a night, I didn't think she would mind the trade-off, considering she'd have the ring of her dreams.

The ring was meant to be a surprise, but I figured it would be better to call her and come clean. How else would I rationalize not returning until the next day?

Calling wasn't that easy. There wasn't a single bar of cellular service at the farm, so I didn't even think to bring my phone on that trip, but I remembered noticing an old princess telephone in Ma's kitchen, and so I thought I'd call the old-fashioned way, using the nearest payphone.

"Golly, I don't think Harpers Ferry has one," replied the first person I asked. "Do they even make payphones anymore?"

I wandered a couple of blocks before I thought to go back to the store. Since the owner called the farm the day before, I was sure that, under the circumstances, he'd be happy to call again. I wanted to catch him before he left for his appointment, but when I got back, the *Yes, we are open!* sign had been flipped, and the *Sorry, we are closed* side glared back at me.

I found another shop that was still open, and the shopkeeper was even able to put her hands on a phonebook. Ethel Marie Winter. At least I remembered her name. There were eight listings for Winter but no Ethel Maries, and the rural route addresses were not helpful.

The shopkeeper was impatient to leave and, as I scoured the pages another time, she drummed her fingers on the counter. I took the hint and left.

By now I was thirsty, and I ducked into The Tankard, the pub where Daisy and I had shared our meager dinner a few nights earlier. This evening, though, I felt prosperous and could afford anything on the menu, so I ordered a steak and started a tab.

When I told the friendly bartender that it was urgent that I call my girlfriend back at the farm, and I couldn't find the number, she offered a solution.

"She's probably listed under Winter's Farm. Everyone around here knows that place," she said, producing a phonebook and a landline.

I was encouraged to find the number listed as she suggested, but the busy signal was discouraging. The line was still busy when I tried again ten minutes later, and, since I didn't want to take advantage of the favor, after finding it still busy during several more attempts, I gave up.

"Hey, man, at least you can tell her you tried," she said.

• • •

The sign on the door of the Lost and Found gave the opening time as eleven, but I'd been pacing in front of the shop since eight o'clock because I believed the owner when he said he

23

would be there first thing in the morning. He was aware that I was in a hurry, and, even though he was doing me a favor, I expected him to show up earlier than eleven.

At ten thirty, he still hadn't arrived, and, had I not paid for it up front, I would have considered leaving. But returning with nothing to show for my disappearance would be more awkward. I wished Ma was telepathic and would pick up that she should explain the situation to Daisy and no longer keep my expedition a secret.

"Oh, good. You came early, too," he said all smiles, when he arrived at ten forty-five.

I was antsy, yet relieved, but when he announced he was going to have to slip away to meet a client until after lunch, I protested.

"Sorry, she's a paying customer," he said, shrugging his shoulders. "I'm sure you understand."

"What about me? Aren't I a p-p-paying customer?"

"Yes, of course, but you must realize that since I'm donating the engraving, you'll have to be a little flexible. Shall we say in an hour?"

"May I at least use your phone to call the farm?" I asked.

"Oh, no. Sorry," he said, "I have to keep this store locked up. We have too many valuables in here as you can see."

I wasn't happy about losing an hour, but at least he nailed down a definite time, and I'd be on my way back to the farm before too long.

I couldn't imagine what was going on in Daisy's head. Whether she learned I lied or not, I couldn't blame her for being angry. But I worried the affair would not put an unnecessary dent in our otherwise perfect relationship.

I killed an hour or so wandering around the town again, and after I got back to the store, I fumed over the waste of time, when I learned the owner had gotten his dates mixed up and had never left.

"So, did you f-f-finish my ring?"

"Oh, my goodness, no. You never told me the names for the inscription. And now I'm afraid I've started something else. But don't worry, I won't be long."

I was furious, but to clear my anger I poked around the store. I'd never heard of a curio shop before, and I soon determined the name didn't differentiate this store from any other secondhand store. The Lost and Found was chock-a-block with random things.

A glass doll with a broken face and big blue eyes stared down at me from atop a cabinet containing a tin tray of old, bent bullets, no doubt used in some sort of historical scuffle. Next to the bullets was a basket of modern sport watches.

One of the most out of place items was a keychain of a kangaroo—half a keychain, actually. It was split down the middle, with a little latch that was meant to attach to the other half, which was missing. The price tag read *Imported from Australia!*

"Would you take a little less for this?" I asked the owner. I hated to bother him, but I wanted to pick it up for the Australian hiker who was working at the farm. I never caught the hiker's name, but I was sure he'd enjoy the joke. "Fifteen dollars seems a b-b-bit steep."

The owner was displeased by the interruption, and his face registered disbelief. "Can't you read? The item came all the way from Australia."

"Yes, but it's not even a f-f-full keychain," I protested. "It's only half."

I coughed up the cash, anyway, knowing full well I was being swindled. As a gag gift, though, it was too good to pass up, and I made a point of insisting the tag indicating its origin be included in the purchase.

The day was slipping by, and I thought hovering next to the man might spur him to work faster. Instead, it only encouraged conversation.

"Can you appreciate how delicate this part is? This is where you have to be good. One slip could ruin everything."

I was frustrated and far less concerned about ruining the ring than about the irreparable damage I could be causing to my relationship with Daisy. At one point, I thought of grabbing the ring, running back to the farm and risking any bad luck it might bring.

It was three o'clock before I flew out of the store with my purchase. I hitched a ride partway and speed-walked the rest, and it was nearly dusk when I arrived.

I saw the familiar sign, but I didn't remember a gate. Not when Daisy and I arrived a few days earlier and not when I left the day before. I wondered if I was even at the right farm. The fence was at least fifteen feet high; yet, through the bars I recognized the giant trees flanking the driveway that stretched a half mile or so to the farmhouse.

The problem wasn't breaking and entering. Ma wouldn't mind that I walked right in. The problem was that I couldn't find the latch. I scratched my head and searched around the sides for another way in.

Had I not stumbled across the half-hidden, faded sign, I might never have noticed the wires that snaked among all the dried-up morning glories and other vines woven into the chain links. *Danger! Electrified Fence.* The words shocked me to attention, and I was relieved that I hadn't followed my first instinct which was to climb over.

I went back to the gate, and after a more thorough search I found a small button set into the frame. I pressed it, presumably to send a signal to the farmhouse. There was a momentary delay before the response came, and the lock clicked open. I slipped through, careful not to let any part of my body touch the fence. Once inside, I used a stick to pull it closed behind me.

Making the long walk down the farm's driveway was a breeze by comparison, and I was relieved at the familiarity of my surroundings. Everything else was as I remembered, and Ma was sitting on the porch. She waved to me as I passed.

"Figured it was you," she hollered. "You were gone longer than you said. Did you get what you went for?"

I patted my pocket. "Yep, and Daisy is going to be very happy."

"I'm sure she will be."

I walked up to the porch. "Say, did you always have that gate? I don't remember one when I left."

"I swear, you city folks! Of course, it was there. I usually keep it wide open, but you had stars in them big, blue eyes of yours when you left, so you probably didn't notice."

"You're right, of course. The gate had to be there. I guess I wasn't paying attention. But, man, that fence is tall!"

"Gotta be to keep them damn deer and coyotes out. They used to make a mess of the henhouse before Pa had the boys put it up."

"Is it really electrified like the sign says? I was afraid to touch."

She batted away a large moth flapping around her face, and it slammed into the wall. We watched it recover from the blow and flutter in a circle over our heads.

"Oh, yeah. We always had one to keep the cattle in, but Pa was worried I'd be out here by myself after he passed on, so he added a few feet...and a few hundred volts. Had to special order some of the parts." She snickered. "It's probably illegal."

"Ha-ha. Ma, you are so funny. But you don't have the electricity turned on now, do you?"

Ma giggled at the crackling sound the moth made when it dive-bombed the bug zapper suspended from the porch ceiling.

"Now? Shouldn't be. It wouldn't be right, what with the farm full of you kids working all over the place and all, and with folks coming and going all the time. Gate's mostly open, 'cept last night. A bunch of wild animals was howling, and I locked the place up tight."

"Good to know. Hey, I can't wait to show the ring to Daisy. Have you seen her?"

"Nope. She was supposed to work with me in the kitchen today, but she never showed up. For what I pay you kids, I hope she was busy doing something." She chuckled. "Check down in the garden."

I thanked her and left.

"I hope you find her. She's such a nice gal. You're a lucky man she chose you."

I wasn't surprised that Ma liked her. Daisy had one of those winning personalities anyone would find appealing, the kind of woman you'd want to introduce to your parents. I felt good, knowing Ma was right. Daisy had chosen me, and I was a very lucky man, indeed.

As I turned to leave, I felt a cold sweat. What did Ma say? That Daisy hadn't shown up for work. Was she ill? As I started to jog, I remembered something else. What the hell did she mean: she *hoped* I'd find Daisy?

The first person I saw in the garden was the guy I'd been working with. He was about six three and heavy with a thick, flaming-red beard, and he was finishing up his work.

"Hey, Red. You sure made a lot of progress while I was gone. I'm gonna check in with Daisy first, and then I'll be back. You can fill me in on where you left off, and what we have to do tomorrow."

Rivers of sweat streamed down his face, but Red acted cool, and he acknowledged me with only a nod as he put away his tools. Most of the other hikers weren't as hardworking as he was. In the adjacent field, Tornado was supposed to be planting pumpkin seeds, but I could see she was goofing off. Without Pa around to do the maintenance, Ma's farm equipment had fallen into disrepair, and she had to rely on hikers to plant thousands of seeds in endless rows by hand.

Pumpkins were Ma's biggest source of income and, to fully mature in time for the Halloween season, she needed all the seeds in the ground by the beginning of June. The faster the deadline approached, the more desperate she became, and she'd offer to pay hikers double to be sure the job got finished on time.

No one planting pumpkins was happy about the assignment. The Australian guy I'd bought the keychain for complained that the constant bending over was backbreaking.

"I didn't come all the way from Australia to be miserable," he'd groused. "But my friend needed the money, and Ma kept offering us these insane amounts of cash to work longer, so here I am."

Daisy gasped when he showed us the thick wad of cash Ma'd paid him. "The deal sounded dodgy to me at first," he'd said, "but she came through on her promise. Gave me this Rolex if I would stay another week, so I guess I'll have to now. It'll just be me, though, because my friend disappeared."

"What do you mean, disappeared?" Daisy had asked him.

The Australian shrugged. "Oh, I'm not worried or anything. He's probably holed up in a local bar somewhere. It's just that I thought we were traveling together. Funny that he took his tent and everything."

Ma had said she was bewildered herself when his friend came to the house for his pay the night before and announced he was leaving unexpectedly.

"I thought something was fishy," the Australian had said. He'd only come to work to be with his friend, and now that he was gone, the Australian was eager to leave. He told her he would finish out the week she'd paid him for, and then take off. "She tried to convince me to stay longer by throwing this piece of jewelry at me." He'd held up a locket. "What am I supposed to do with this? She said it was valuable."

"I think it's beautiful," Daisy had told him. "I'd buy it from you if I had the money."

"Here ya go. Knock yourself out." Just like that, he gave it to Daisy.

"I hope you find your friend," I'd said, but he didn't seem comforted.

"Yeah, thanks. I'm going to hang around for the rest of the week to see if he shows up. If he doesn't, I'll probably leave. Hey, keep a lookout for him, will you? He's a big guy, and his arms are covered with stupid tattoos. You can't miss him."

I hadn't seen the tattooed guy anywhere since, but I thought I'd stop by the Australian's tent to give him the gag gift I picked up in the curio shop. But, as I neared the campground, I was surprised to see that he must have left early, because his tent was gone.

More shocking was that my own tent was missing, too. It wasn't as though I didn't remember where I'd pitched it. Daisy and I had been living in the tent for almost a week. I couldn't fathom why it was gone, and I was desperate to find it.

I had a horrible thought and my heart pounded. Had she left me? We'd never even had an argument before, so the simplest explanation was that she'd moved it somewhere else.

I was frantic and I searched everywhere, but our tent simply wasn't there.

"What the hell? Where's my tent? And where's Daisy?"

3

Daisy

Daisy couldn't see. The hood over her head made that impossible. *Is it a pillowcase?* It was soft like one and sheer enough to distinguish between darkness and light. Whatever the material, having it over her head made breathing tricky, especially with the gag in her mouth. The pungent omnipresent odor of mothballs wasn't enough of a clue to where she was being held. *Why is this happening to me? And how long am I going to be kept here?*

She remembered not sleeping that last night in her tent and blamed it on the howling sounds off to the north, but a pack of scrapping coyotes wasn't the only reason she'd tossed and turned. It was finding out that Strider had lied to her, and she was convinced he'd gone and wasn't coming back, leaving her alone and bewildered.

That morning he'd told her Ma asked him to run some errands and that he wouldn't be gone long. By afternoon, she wondered what was taking so long. When he still hadn't returned to eat the dinner she'd cooked, she was annoyed. As the sky grew dark her irritation turned to worry. She dashed to the house assuming Ma would know his status, and what she learned only made things worse.

"Errands? I never sent him on any errands. Sounds to me like he told you a big, fat story."

Daisy's heart sank. "Well, where do you think he is? He couldn't have left. All his stuff is still here."

"How would I know? Nobody tells me anything. I hope you don't expect me to pay him for today, since he wasn't even here." She sounded firm. "Now, be on your way. I got to get my beauty sleep."

Ma was right about the time. The other hikers were already in their tents when Daisy got back to hers. After sleeping beside Strider for almost a week, she had forgotten what it was like not to have a tent mate, and she only went through the motions of going to sleep. In no time, her imagination took over and kept her awake as she agonized over why he'd left her.

Coyotes wailing in the distance added to the eeriness and tension, and when the racket became too much to tolerate, she pulled down the zipper of her door flap and stared outside into the blackness. The beam of her flashlight was dim, and she couldn't remember the last time she'd replaced the batteries. She smacked it against the ground, and it got brighter.

In the distance, she saw a figure standing near the vegetable plots. "What are you doing out here?" she asked when she got within earshot.

"Oh, hi," said Red, setting down his shovel. "Ma said if I kept track of my hours, I could work as much as I wanted, and, boy, digging sure is cooler at night." He saw she was shaking. "Are you okay?"

"Not really. Being over there in my tent all by myself is seriously freaking me out."

"Mine's big enough for two, and you're welcome to stay with me tonight." Before she could reject the idea, he held up his hands. "There would be no funny business, just so you know."

She would have preferred an offer from a female hiker, like that girl she'd worked with in the kitchen; yet, part of her was relieved to be bunking with someone so physically strong. She went to get her sleeping bag and a small kit of essentials.

Red stayed true to his word by minding his own business. He fell asleep right away and, even though he snored lightly, Daisy found the sound of another person next to her comforting. Soon she dozed off, until her bladder screamed her awake a few hours later.

Careful not to wake Red, she left his tent as quietly as she could and dashed for the outhouse. She was halfway there when she realized she'd forgotten her flashlight, but her mission was urgent and she knew it would be dumb to turn back. She kept her eyes focused on the outhouse nightlight, so she wouldn't become freaked out by shadows.

She was finishing up when the coyotes started up again. This time they sounded closer, and she was terrified and grateful for the small bulb that lit the inside. Hiding in the outhouse all night was her least favorite option, so she drew on a calming, yogic, deep-breathing practice while she devised a plan to get back to the safety of Red's tent. She was confident he would protect her.

As soon as she unlatched and cracked open the door, a thin muzzle streaked with grey and red fur poked into the space. It started sniffing and scared any calmness she managed to conjure right out of her. Somehow, though, she kept from screaming.

She hoped the animal couldn't see her standing behind the door, though she was fairly certain it could smell her. And when he nosed forward a little more, she knew she had to act fast or the animal would soon be inside the outhouse.

But, she caught it by surprise when she made a fist and bashed down on its head, stunning it long enough for her to slam the door shut. The coyote cried out, and the blow made him more aggressive. He butted his head harder against the

34

door. Each time she tried to slide the latch in place, the beast would shove its nose back in, making the door impossible to secure.

At last, she was able to slam her back up against the door long enough to get it locked. Finally, the beast whimpered and went away, but she remained in the outhouse for another hour before she thought it safe to make a run for Red's tent.

Once she heard a park ranger describe the way coyotes often shadow humans and, as she stepped out into the shadows, it wasn't a comforting memory. But, it was her last thought before someone hit her over the head and knocked her unconscious.

Now, bound and gagged, she struggled to recall any detail of the person who attacked her. If Strider had been there, she kept thinking, he would have protected her.

Strider! What the hell happened to him? He was everything she sought in a man and thought she would never find. He was unassuming, completely natural, and self-effacing, not to mention tall and handsome, the complete opposite from the guy she'd ended it with a few weeks earlier.

She was convinced her luck had changed. Strider loved her spunk and spontaneity and, unlike her ex, he wasn't mean, jealous, or controlling. In fact, once she leveled with him about the extent of her hiking skills, he'd been more than willing to have her push *him* around a little, confident that things would get done a lot faster.

Once, she even saved him from a disastrous fall. They were hiking a difficult part of the trail, and he'd been following close behind, enjoying the view and not paying attention to where she had been carefully placing her feet.

She was experienced enough to understand that one wrong step could send either one of them tumbling down the mountain face. As she eased over a thick tree that crossed the muddy path, her foot slipped.

She called back, "Hey! Be careful when you get to this—"

All she heard was a snap and a shout, "Whoa!"

She turned back to see his foot sliding downwards in the mud and his arms wind-milling as he attempted to regain his balance and keep from teetering off over empty air.

"Hang on!" She planted her feet and grabbed one of his flailing arms. She was strong, but he was much taller and outweighed her by at least fifty pounds. For a moment, she didn't think her grip would hold, but his life was at stake. She wrapped a leg around a tree for support and grabbed him with her other hand, pulling him back to safety.

"Jesus, you s-s-saved my life," he gasped. "You're one awesome lady."

As the hands she used to save his life now ached from being tied together, she hoped he'd be able to return the favor.

4

My heart was pounding as I sped back to the garden. It was bad enough that all my stuff and tent were missing, now all I could think about was Daisy. I went straight to Red to ask if he had any information, and I had more trouble than ever getting out the words. In addition to my stutter, I was breathless.

Red only shrugged. "I haven't seen your tent, but Daisy? Hmm. There's a Daisy the next bed over." He pointed at a hole I'd dug earlier. The painted, wooden sign stuck in the ground read *Daisy's Dill.*

I raised my voice and no doubt came across as angry. "No, not D-D-Daisy's vegetable bed, the real Daisy."

"Hey, chill, man! I'm only trying to help." He took his time to think. "Which one is Daisy? I forget."

Jesus, how could he not know? I didn't want to take the time to describe her, because I was in a hurry, and it was obvious to me he wasn't going to be much help.

I caught Tornado resting against a tree on the other side. Her shirt was dark with sweat, and I gathered she was taking a break from work.

"Howdy. You engaged yet?"

"Not even c-c-close."

Tornado apologized for not being helpful. She had been on pumpkin seed duty all day, so she didn't run across Daisy, and she advised me to ask the tall girl in the garden, who'd spent time with Daisy the day before.

The girl was pretty with shapely legs and a tiny waist, and she was using a cultivator like a pro, wiping beads of sweat off her forehead. She leaned on her hoe. Freckles crossed her nose and cheeks and her curly red hair ran wild in every direction. Unlike Daisy, she was almost my height so, eye to eye, I could see her gray eyes clearly.

"What's up?" She was breathless.

I was frantic and perhaps too abrupt. "Hey, I'm trying to find my girlfriend. Kind of short, dark hair. Goes by Daisy or Daisy Duck. Have you seen her?"

"Daisy Duck? Cute name, isn't it? Yeah, I think her tent is over—" She gestured to the empty space. "Weird. Last time I checked it was there."

"Let's forget about the tent for a minute. Have you seen *her* lately?"

"I don't think so, but I guess it depends on what you mean by 'lately.' Yesterday, she and I helped Ma in the kitchen. Maybe she's with her."

"No, she's not. I just left there. Ma told me she might be here."

"Well, maybe you passed each other."

I was about to run back up to the house. "So, you must be the other girl Daisy was telling me about?"

"Other girl? Don't you remember me? I'm Rachel."

"Rachel. Okay. Got it. Thanks." While I did recognize her face from the day before, I'd only seen her for an instant and I didn't remember learning her name.

When I entered the kitchen, Ma was leaning against the sink, her goofy cane on standby next to her. She was busy picking through mounds of strawberries, tossing the best ones into little tins. With Daisy's assistance, she planned to turn the berries into her famous jam. Crude labels bearing a sketch of the farmhouse lay in a stack, waiting to be affixed to the jars, and I was able to make out the block letters: *Sally's Strawberries.*

"Ma, I'm f-f-freaking out. Daisy's not d-d-down in the garden. I can't find her anywhere."

"Hmm. Slow down now. You're all excited and talking kind of funny again. Listen, I thought I told you I didn't know where she was." She didn't look up from what she was doing. "She was supposed to be here helping me with these dang berries."

"Well, nobody at the campsite has seen her, and my tent is gone, and all our stuff is missing."

"Land sakes! That's not good. Weren't you two getting hitched or something?"

"Yes, which is why I went to town. To buy the ring, remember?"

"Yeah, I remember you told me."

"So, you didn't see her leave, did you?" I asked. "I mean, I can't believe she would."

"She'd be the first one to leave without getting paid if she did, so I bet she's around here somewhere."

"But where? Can you try to think of anything else that might help me?"

"Now that I think of it, I believe she did come up here right around dinner time." When Ma sorted the last berry, she shoved aside the empty box and started picking through a full one. "Asked if you was back from getting me supplies or something. I told her I couldn't imagine what she was talking about." She winked. "I wasn't supposed to tell her about the ring, was I? I thought your little trip was a secret."

"No, yeah, but damn, now D-D-Daisy knows I lied to her. She probably thinks I left her and wasn't coming back."

Ma shrugged. "Or, maybe when you didn't come back, she left."

"Left? No, no. She would never do that. Daisy loves me. It was her idea to get m-m-married in the first place."

"Well, I sure wouldn't have let Pa get away with treating me like that."

I paced around the kitchen, thinking how much things were screwed up because of that damned ring. I was almost afraid to ask her if she knew what happened to my tent. Even if she were angry and left me, it was inconceivable that she would take my stuff with her.

"Maybe she wasn't the only one who thought you weren't coming back. One of the other hikers could have taken your stuff. I have no idea where it is. Hard enough to keep track of my own. In fact, have you seen the key to my storeroom?"

I asked one more time. "You said yourself she was p-p-robably still around here. You must have some idea?"

Ma waved around the kitchen. "Well, she sure as heck ain't in here. Maybe she ran off with that Australian guy. Haven't seen him in a while. Women always fall for a man with an accent. She fell for you, after all, and you kind of have an accent, no offense."

I wasn't convinced Daisy had abandoned me, and I trusted Ma but I also thought that she was being naïve. If I poked around in the house, I thought I might find a clue. I asked to use her bathroom under the guise that the weather was warming up and the outhouse was getting stuffy. She was more than happy to oblige.

"Could I use the one upstairs? I'd like a little privacy if you know what I mean."

When I got there, I had something else in mind: to check out every room. To throw her off guard, I flipped the bathroom light on and closed the door from the hall before I tiptoed around.

Maybe it was due to her bad leg and lack of mobility, but Ma clearly wasn't much of a housekeeper. The entire upstairs was incredibly dusty, and there were cobwebs in every corner.

The first rooms appeared set up for guests. Towels were folded neatly on the bed and the sheets were turned down. It could have been a B&B if not for the two tiny corn husk dolls tucked under the covers, their creepy heads resting on the pillows. They didn't have eyes, but it felt like they were staring at me. I shivered and closed the door. The next five rooms looked exactly like the first. Only one was locked, which I presumed was Ma's.

Finding no traces of Daisy or our stuff, I flushed the toilet and headed back downstairs. On my way back, I found myself in the laundry room, where a pile of clothes heaped on a table caught my attention. Thick, shiny, brown stains that looked stiff and dry were splattered across a flannel shirt thrown on the top, but when I touched it, a splash of reddish liquid came off on my finger. Was it blood?

"I hope you don't think I've got your girlfriend stashed around here," Ma said, scaring me half to death. Then she cackled. "Can't believe you didn't hear me. With my old cane I clunk around louder than Pa's old tractor. And don't think I didn't hear you snooping around upstairs, neither."

"I'm sorry. I thought I might find a clue or something, I'm desperate."

"There's nothing up there now. Haven't been in those rooms much since Pa died. The place used to be crawling with young'uns. And, once we ran a B&B, too, but folks that came to stay were too wild, so I put an end to it."

Before I could ask about the "young'uns," she continued, "I see you found Sparky's shirt. I swear, that boy is the clumsiest fool, always getting scratched up. Luckily, ol' Ma here knows a thing or two about washing out blood stains."

So, I was right. I dropped Sparky's shirt and ran my hands over my pants to wipe off any traces of his blood.

"Weird," I said, on our way back to the kitchen. "I didn't think he ever wore a shirt."

Ma sighed. "And this is exactly why. Every time he puts one on, he manages to ruin it."

"You know a lot about him. How long has he been working here?"

"A while now. He doesn't seem to want to leave." She went back to her berry project.

I apologized again for snooping around. In fact, I was ashamed, but every lead hit a dead end. Short of searching the entire farm, I was running out of ideas. I tried changing my line of questioning.

"Can you remember the last time you saw her?" I could tell she was thinking it over.

"Give me a minute. Yeah, it was late last night."

"Wait, you saw her last night? Before or after dinner?" Dragging out information bit by bit was frustrating, but I felt I was getting somewhere. "Where was she? What was she doing?"

"You might ask the big guy with all the red hair. Pretty sure I seen 'em together."

"Red? Are you sure?" Her comment landed like a ton of bricks. "I just sp-sp-spoke to him a few minutes ago, and he claimed he didn't recognize her name."

At last, she looked up from her work. She wore a wicked little smile. "That's not what I heard."

"What? What's that supposed to mean?" I was furious, but before I could send forth a string of expletives the wind-up kitchen timer made a ding.

Without giving me an answer, she grabbed her cane and lumbered over to the enormous stove. Wearing oversized mitts, she pulled a giant pan out of one of the ovens.

"Lasagna's done!"

5

I bolted out the kitchen door. I hadn't gotten the answers I wanted. My stomach turned at the thought that Daisy and Red had fooled around. If anything, what Ma had said made it worse, and I was more confused than ever. And heartbroken. Yet, I was encouraged that she'd seen Daisy late the night before. But since it was unlikely that Daisy would have set out alone in the dark, I had a feeling that Ma was right. Maybe she was still on the farm.

While I didn't consider him a friend, we had slaved a couple of days together, and I thought we'd gotten along fine. If he and Daisy slept together, it would at least explain why he played dumb with me earlier and pretended not to know who she was. I was steaming mad and marched over to the garden to get some straight answers.

I thought about the day we'd arrived at the farm. Red was the only one working and seemed glad to have another guy to help. With the Australian off planting pumpkins, Red had been doing all the heavy work by himself.

I remembered when Ma came down to give me instructions on how to make her raised beds. They had to be exactly eighty-four inches long by thirty-six inches wide and forty-eight inches deep. She even gave us yardsticks, so our measurements would be precise.

"Makin' vegetable beds is like fixin' lasagna," she'd instructed. "There's a system."

Lasagna. There it was again.

"After you dig down forty-eight inches, put down a layer of loose soil, yea thick. Then a layer of compost, same depth.

Make sure they're nice and smooth. Do another layer of soil on top of the compost and then another layer of compost. Got it?"

I asked an innocent question and got slammed. "Do the d-d-dimensions have to be exact?"

"Lookie here, son. I didn't win all them blue ribbons being sloppy. Nope, our beds are always this size. Always have been, always will be. Should of wrote a book about it."

As she left, she heaved an exaggerated sigh, and grumbled about how tiresome it was to explain things over and over to her ever-changing workforce.

There were dozens of beds, evenly aligned in rows of six each. Some of them were currently producing crops like the strawberries Ma was making into jam. Plots like those only needed a slight weeding. The season was over for crops on some of the other beds, and they required time-consuming but not particularly strenuous renovations. It was digging new ones from scratch that was so laborious.

I remembered thinking four feet wouldn't be that hard to dig until I learned that all the regular shovel handles were broken, and I'd be using a narrow spade. Once we dug the main trench, though, the rest of her system was easy to complete, especially since the worst part was cheerfully done by a goofy and talkative kid named Sparky—the same Sparky with the bloody T-shirt in Ma's laundry room.

His job was to walk the wheelbarrow full of compost all the way from the smelly pile at the far side of the next field and dump it near the new beds we were preparing. While we spread the stinky stuff into the beds, Sparky would go back for another load, but not before talking our ears off.

"Here's some of Ma's secret sauce. Well, I guess I better go back and get more. This is hard work, you know, the back and forth. And her compost is heavy, you know, and the ground is so bumpy. So much falls out on the way. I could get a bunch of loads just from what spills. But, you know, I don't mind. I'd rather do this than dig. Diggin's hard."

Sparky claimed you'd never catch him wearing a shirt until Christmas, and his wiry and sunburned torso and arms were covered with scratches. Some of the more gnarly scabs were yellow and oozed a little pus. Anyone who spent time in his company knew better than to bring up the subject, because he never needed encouragement to ramble on and on. He accounted for each scratch the way some people describe their tattoos.

"Oh, these? This one I got when I tripped and fell down up at Jefferson Rock. And these ugly ones I got over there, I think. No, they were from a bush out back. Probably one of those Barberry bushes. Gross, huh? Now this one—"

Sparky would eventually leave, and even though the compost heap was a good ten or fifteen-minute walk each way, sometimes he'd be gone for an hour or more, which was fine with us. He could be away as long as he wanted.

Ma warned us against filling the beds too high. "Just put down four layers for now, like I said. When we figure out what we're going to plant where, I'll know what to put in next."

The other person working with us that day was Tornado. For someone named after something so powerful, she was incredibly weak. In the time it took her to cultivate one bed—which she proudly proclaimed would be for Tornado's Tomatoes—Red and I had weeded four between us. We worked side by side that entire day only taking breaks for water. Unlike Sparky, he was not the talkative sort, but that was about to change, because I needed answers.

I ran to his tent, "Hey, Red! Come out here. I need to t-t-talk to you."

He took his time and was frowning when he emerged. Standing straight, he was taller than me by a couple inches.

"What's your problem?" he growled.

"Ma told me you were with my g-g-girlfriend last night. How come you lied to me?"

"Slow down, fella. First of all, she never said she was your girlfriend."

"Oh, come on. She didn't have to. Everyone knew we were a couple!"

"Well, I didn't. Anyway, nothing happened, so what's the big deal?"

"Hey, asshole, it's a b-b-big deal because I don't like other guys fooling around with her. Also, because she happens to be missing, along with my tent and all the rest of my stuff. And you were the last p-p-person to see her. That's why."

Red was tall and solid even before he got puffed up with rage, but his size didn't deter Rachel. Before Red and I had a chance to start swinging, she stepped between us.

"Okay, ladies! You're both gorgeous, and I'm sure every woman on the planet would kill to go out with you. But can we focus now?" She faced me. "Red said nothing happened, so let's start there." Then she turned to Red. "And Strider has a serious problem here and needs our help."

We both backed down, and I stuck out my hand to apologize for what was probably an overreaction.

"When Ma told me you and Daisy were together, I imagined the worst and may have freaked out a little. So, I'm s-s-sorry. But, I'm out of my mind. I don't know where she is, and nobody else does, either."

Again, Rachel took charge. "Come on, if we put our heads together, she should be easy enough to find. I mean, think about it. She was here last night, and she's not here now. Red, you saw her last. Tell us what happened."

"All right, but I can't be sure I was the last one to see her. Besides, he's not going to like what I'm going to say." He shuffled his feet and stared at the ground.

"Go on," Rachel said.

"So, I was working late when Daisy stopped by and said she wanted to talk. Long story short, she was scared out of her mind. Her tent was on the other side, all by itself, and she told me it made her nervous."

I knew that it was my fault for thinking we needed more privacy, and we probably pitched it too far from the others. The farm was very dark at night and full of wildlife, and while the sounds hadn't bothered us before, I understood her concern. I felt terrible that poor Daisy had no way of knowing I would be delayed.

"Well, she must have been very scared, because she asked if she could sleep with me."

"She what? You told me n-n-nothing happened!"

"Relax, nothing did. She was so frightened, I said it was okay as long as she stayed on her side."

I put my head in my hands. "God, you're making this so hard for me."

Rachel put an arm around me. "Go on, Red. What about today? What did you guys do first thing this morning?"

"That's just it. She wasn't in my tent when I woke up. I can't be positive, but I believe she left in the middle of the night."

"Do you think she l-l-left the farm?"

"In the middle of the night? I don't think so. She was too scared."

"All right, all right," said Rachel. She's not here, so why don't we start by searching the rest of the farm? I'll see who I can round up to help, and we'll fan out."

Sparky was nowhere to be found, but she managed to snag Tornado. Since she was working pumpkin seed detail, she was happy to do something more interesting. Rachel had devised a plan, and after she sent the others off to search in different directions, it was just the two of us. With a pat on the shoulder, she told me not to worry, that she'd help me find her. We'd only met, but I already had a good feeling about her. I'd been depressed and defeated, and Rachel was smart and quick and helpful, and exactly what I needed.

She even had two flashlights.

6

Winter's Farm was far from picture perfect. Without Pa around to do the upkeep, the barns and sheds in the central area surrounding the aging farmhouse had fallen into disrepair, and while hikers meticulously maintained the raised vegetable beds, the rest of the garden was overgrown and shabby. The number of acres under production had shrunk to few than the dozen or so that encircled the house, and the layout created a false sense of intimacy.

In fact, the property was quite large. Cattle once grazed and crops flourished in extensive fields that stretched out from the farmhouse in all directions. Now abandoned, they were left to the whims of nature and under the control of scrub bushes, trees, and volunteer vegetation. There were steep hills and lowlands, and in previously arable land, rocks and boulders somehow worked their way up to the surface to dominate the landscape.

Much of the property was heavily forested, surrounded by thick woods on all sides. Those natural borders, together with the electric fence, insured that this sense of intimacy was guarded for maximum privacy.

After a long day of hard work, hikers generally gathered around the campfire, and few ever ventured outside the immediate vicinity of the working acreage, so the bulk of the property was unexplored.

The farther from the campsite we walked, the more naive I felt it was to think that simply "fanning out" was sufficient direction for such a daunting challenge. A couple of amateurs, unfamiliar with the vast amount of ground we needed to cover, trying to locate a missing person in the dark was not an efficient search party model. But it was all we had.

I was preoccupied, but Rachel didn't seem to mind walking without speaking. We stopped now and then to scour the landscape for clues in the dim light, and after twenty minutes or so she broke the silence and asked me to tell her a little about Daisy.

"What do you mean? What do you want to know?"

"Oh, I'm not sure. Anything we can use. In the movies, the more detectives learn about the guys they're tracking down, the quicker they find them. So, what's she like?"

"Well, she's the sweetest, kindest—"

"No. Of course, she wouldn't be your girlfriend if she wasn't all those things. Let me put it another way. What does she like to do?"

"That's easy, too. The only thing I've ever done with her is hike and camp, and I know she likes those."

"Nothing else?" Her voice had a little smile in it. "Never mind, I'm sorry, too personal. So, what you're saying is she wouldn't have minded crossing some of this rough terrain we're in now."

I ignored her previous question. "Not at all."

"How about those woods? They look a little menacing. Would she have been afraid to go in there?"

"I wouldn't have thought so before, but now I'm not so sure. She was afraid to be alone in our tent, don't forget."

"Yeah, according to Red." She didn't elaborate. "But maybe she did go in there and got lost."

"In any case, why would she be out here? It doesn't make sense."

We approached a steep hill and as we started to climb, Rachel made another attempt at conversation and asked me to tell her about Daisy's family. I felt foolish, because we'd gotten so caught up in ourselves in the heat of our newfound passion, we never talked about them. I wondered how I hadn't been interested enough to ask.

"Hmm. A little odd, don't you think, for two people who are engaged?" she asked.

I stopped walking. "Hey, what makes you think w-w-we were engaged? Did she tell you?"

"No, maybe. I don't know. I guess I assumed you were. The ring and all. Are you?"

"No. Getting engaged was more her idea, and I sort of went along and f-f-figured we'd take one step at a time." I turned the question around and asked if she had any information about Daisy that might be helpful.

"Well, I'm not her fiancé, so I'm not sure how useful I can be."

She waited a moment to gauge my reaction to the joke. I did think it was funny, but I suppressed a laugh. After all, my question had been serious. Rachel was the other woman Daisy described working with her, and I knew women liked to share. I needed to learn if Daisy had told her anything that might give us a clue.

"Daisy had me in sti-sti-stitches talking about your adventures up there in the kitchen. She said Ma was quite the character."

"Gee, I didn't find anything funny at all. I was terrified. I didn't know the first thing about canning, not even that people use jars. I thought you canned in cans. Next to Daisy, I was a lost cause. She could chop up stuff like one of those super chefs on television."

"Wait, I'm confused. She told me you were the p-p-pro."

"Me? Are you kidding? I'm an outdoorsy kind of gal. In the kitchen, I'm all thumbs."

I kept listening, but my face lost its smile as Rachel explained how inept she was with a knife, and that Ma had taken her off chopping duty to do some lettering on the jar labels. After she finished the labels, she hand-painted signs for the vegetables she and Daisy were going to plant.

"Wow. What you describe is exactly the opposite of h-h-how Daisy said things transpired. She told me you were the pro, and she did the sign painting. Perhaps I heard her wrong."

Rachel touched my hand. "But back to your question. What I do recall is that she really knows her way around a kitchen, almost as though she'd been there before. Had she?"

"Not to my knowledge."

When Rachel suggested that Daisy was perhaps just one of those people who were good at knowing where things were supposed to be kept, it didn't ring true. I thought back to one of our first nights together and an incident that was humorous at the time. Daisy was rooting around in her bag forever, in search of a hair clip. Usually, she pulled her hair back into a quick knot, but the humidity had various strands poking out around her head, and she wanted something to hold it down. She checked every nook and cranny before I pointed out that she was holding the clip in her hand.

"I remember her saying she could never remember where she put things. Now, I'm beginning to w-w-wonder if you and I are talking about the same woman."

As we neared the top of the hill, Rachel's flashlight revealed a rickety fence that surrounded a small graveyard. The hand-painted sign on the sagging gate read *Winter Family Cemetery*. The graves were organized in an even grid like the farm's garden, with hand-painted wooden markers staked into the ground at the head of each grave.

"Cool!" Rachel said. "I read that in the old days people had personal cemeteries, but I've never seen one."

It was very dark, and we weren't any closer to finding Daisy, and, as much as an old graveyard was something we would have liked to explore, I said we needed to head back. Rachel didn't mind, and she agreed to keep searching again in the morning. As we started back, something caught our eyes—a fresh grave with rich, wet, brown dirt on top, not more than a few days old. Rachel had been working side by side with Ma every day, and Ma never mentioned a thing to her about a service, so perhaps the grave was older than it appeared.

Ma didn't seem to have much of a family, and we considered the funeral could have been a simple, private affair. The marker was odd, though. *Aunt Sally*. No last name, no dates, nothing.

"Speaking of names, I'm curious. What's Daisy's real name?"

"Her real name? You m-m-mean like her last name?"

"I don't care, last name, first name. Didn't you tell me she sometimes went by Daisy Duck? Sounds like a trail name to me. I mean, Strider isn't your real name, is it?"

I stopped walking. She must have thought I was a total loser not to know the real name of my own almost fiancée. Thank god it was dark, and she couldn't see my face. It would have been red from embarrassment.

"I always called her D-D-Daisy."

"Look, maybe Daisy is her real name. I mean, I don't use a trail name. Why would I? I'm just plain Rachel."

Rachel was anything but plain, but I kept my mouth shut and kept walking. When we stopped a few minutes later to get our bearings, she almost crossed a line. "Was she good in bed?"

"What?"

"I'm sorry. Scratch that. Forget I ever asked. It was going to be a joke, but it obviously backfired."

After the inappropriate question, the next few minutes dragged on in silence until we neared the tents, and she broke the tension.

"Fingers crossed that someone's found something, huh Strider?"

"Or s-s-someone."

Red boasted that he covered most of the area to the north, and I was dispirited to learn he'd seen nothing, He said he only had time to walk along the edge of the dense woods on the farm's north boundary. Because it was so dark, he thought it pointless to go in. Besides, he didn't imagine her wanting to wander in there.

It was late and my fantasy of seeing Daisy running toward me across a field, smiling and then jumping into the safety of my arms was crushed when the last person came back empty-handed. Tornado had been running, and we were concerned to see blood on her arms, neck, and shoulders. She was using her sweatshirt to dab at the cuts.

She waved away our worries as she caught her breath. "I got hooked on some damned barbed wire and it hurts like hell. If I hadn't been going so fast, I probably wouldn't have run into it."

Rachel had sent Tornado east past the pumpkin patch field because she was familiar with the area. She intended to start down a path she remembered seeing at the far side, but the entrance was practically invisible in the dark.

"I found an old cabin deep in the woods," she said. "It appeared abandoned, at least from the outside. There wasn't a light inside, you know, from candles or anything, and I didn't even consider that someone could be living there, until I got nearer and called out Daisy's name. That's when I heard a loud crash.

"At first, I thought I'd scared an animal inside, but then a ferocious sounding dog started to snarl out back. From the clanking, I could tell it was on a chain, and I didn't stick around to find out how long it was.

"I wanted to get out of there fast, and I made a quick decision not to go back the way I came. Instead I tried a shortcut, which ended up being a big mistake, because I ran into the barbed wire."

"Do you think D-D-Daisy was inside the cabin?" I asked, heartened by the possibility.

"I can't be sure. All I know is somebody or something in there knocked something over when I called her name."

Rachel wanted Tornado to take us there, but Tornado was exhausted and begged off. She wasn't even sure she could find the place again in the dark, but she offered to try in the morning, with one provision.

"Tell you what. I'll take you close enough to see the place, but I'm not going any farther if that dog's there. And you'll have to wake me up, okay? I'm dead."

"We'll try looking there first," Rachel said when Tornado left. "And, even if she's not there, she's got to be around here somewhere. Isn't the whole property fenced in?"

"Yeah, in fact, I just learned the f-f-fence is electrified."

"Creepy. Who has one of those?"

"Well, Ma does, and she turned it on last night. Something about k-k-keeping out animals."

"She might have a point. I guess you didn't hear those coyotes last night. They were making quite a racket." She paused. "I just thought of something. If the fence was on, Daisy couldn't possibly have gotten out, and that proves she's still in here somewhere."

What she said made sense, but I was frazzled by then and wanted to go to bed. I headed for my tent, until I realized I didn't have a place to sleep anymore.

"You can sleep with me for a night," Rachel said from behind me. "But, remember, you stay on your side, and I'll stay on mine, okay?"

7

Moving a body was hard work. They were always heavier than they looked. At least when they were dead, they didn't fight back. It was when they struggled, that was a real pain.

Someone else had dug the hole previously, and since it was close by, even in the dark it didn't take long to drag the body over. If you stripped off the clothes first, it was a piece of cake. A naked body cuts down on friction, and arms and legs don't get caught on things as easily. The corpse fell to the bottom of the pit with a hard thud. Crap! Why did they always have to land face down? A body needed to be laid out properly, facing up, arms folded and all.

The first shovel of dirt only covered the feet. Much more was needed to pack tightly around the sides. A finger twitched, and one eye struggled to open. *Can't have that. Wouldn't want a half-dead person to get up and start wandering around.* The next shovel full filled the gaping mouth and covered the eyes, and more dirt got stuffed into the nostrils for good measure.

It was time for a nice thick layer of homemade compost and another layer of dirt. Then another layer of each, topped off with a layer of potting soil in a nice smooth finish. It was important to follow the system to the letter.

8

I wasn't quite awake, and not quite asleep, either. Cozy, though. Warm and cozy. The body next to me was soft and I rolled over to wrap an arm around her midsection. She let out a purr of approval and nuzzled my chest. When I tilted my face to drop a kiss on her head, red curls poked back at my face.

"Oh my God!" I cried out, pushing away from her. "Rachel! I'm so sorry! I thought you were Daisy!"

She laughed and rolled back over. "I was half asleep anyway. But do us both a favor and go hit the shower, will you?" She pinched her nose. "You're starting to smell like Sparky. While you're gone, I'll wake up Tornado."

Embarrassed, I dragged myself out of her tent and crossed over to the communal shower in my bare feet. I returned a second later, when I remembered I didn't have any of my stuff. But Rachel was ready with a bar of soap, some shampoo, and even a towel waiting for me outside the tent.

No wonder I stank. The last shower I took was days ago. The water wasn't exactly warm, but I took my time. After everything I'd been through, it felt good to stand in the stream with my head hung back and my eyes closed. I was thankful for the peace and quiet.

"Tornado's gone!" Rachel shouted over the privacy enclosure.

"What do you mean, gone?"

"I mean, she's gone! No tent, nothing."

I was a little sleep deprived, and though Rachel tried to make my bed as comfortable for me as she could, it took me a long time to fall asleep. Rachel, however, was one of those individuals with the gift. She could sleep anywhere, anytime, in any position. Waking up at the same time meant that she was firing on all cylinders, and I wasn't. So, I needed a moment to process the news. Tornado was… gone? Just like that?

When I stepped out, I was surprised to see Sparky waiting to step in.

"Oh, you shower early, too?" he asked. "Man, I'm up here every day, and I've never seen you. Hardly anyone—"

Rachel came to my rescue when she cut him off with the excuse that we needed to go find Tornado.

"Tornado?" Sparky asked. "Isn't she still over—" He stopped talking when he saw that her tent was gone. "Huh. I saw her last night."

Rachel and I had started to slink away, trying to avoid a lengthy conversation, but when he made that last comment, we froze.

"You saw her last n-n-night?" I asked. "Where?"

He explained that Tornado felt guilty about not being helpful the day before, and she wanted to make another trip to that cabin. She hoped to find Daisy, or at least a clue to her whereabouts.

"But on the way a couple more coyotes started to wail, and she totally lost it! She ran off and I couldn't find her anywhere. My guess is that she ended up at that cabin."

Rachel groaned. "So, what you're saying is that to find Tornado we have to locate the cabin. But to find the cabin, we need to locate Tornado."

Sparky laughed. "Kind of a pickle, huh?"

Despite our worries, Rachel and I were able to share a laugh on the way back to her tent. We agreed the compost pile had to be pretty potent if Sparky showered every day and smelled the way he did. We could still hear him talking when the water came back on.

I was still stuck on my dilemma. "Don't you find it weird that the one person who knew the cabin's location is missing?"

Rachel laughed and gave my shoulder a playful push. "Stop being so dramatic. I'm sure there must be a plausible explanation. Tornado can't be the only one who knows where it is. We could always ask Ma."

Talking to Ma meant waking her up, but it was an emergency. She was wearing a nightgown and pink curlers in her hair when she let us in. After apologizing for the intrusion, I told her that we had another problem. Another hiker had disappeared.

"Disappeared? That sounds drastic," she said, plopping her feet up on the chair next to her. "Now, which one is Tornado? I'm trying to place him."

"Tornado's a she, but that's not important right now."

"Might not be important to you, but it is to me. Especially if she's planting my pumpkin seeds."

"Okay, look, she's blonde and skinny and not too tall."

"What is it about your friends always disappearing?" She used her cane to walk over to the stove and pour a cup. "Coffee, anyone?"

I went on to describe how we'd searched for Daisy the night before. I told her about the shack Tornado'd found, and the dog that had scared her away.

"Since it's the only place we haven't searched, we think it's possible that Daisy is there, but T-T-Tornado is the only one who can show us where it is, and she's nowhere to be found."

"Have you seen her?" Rachel asked.

"No, but I bet she's halfway to Harpers Ferry by now. Paid her late last night, in fact. She made a lot of cash off me, that one. Between us, she worked two weeks at double pay. No, I think it was triple."

"So, you're saying she left? Why would she do that? Yesterday, she told me she was staying another few days. She even asked Rachel and me to wake her this morning."

"It was a shock and disappointment to me, too." She brought out a tray of biscuits from a cupboard. "Of course, now that I think of it, I don't see how she could have left. You know, with the fence being on and all."

"Wait a minute. So, is Tornado here or not? You've got me confused," I said.

"How so?"

"It's how you explained away Daisy's d-d-disappearance. You said she wasn't here, but that she couldn't have left."

"I thought you said you found her."

"He thinks she might be locked in that cabin," Rachel said. "If so, we need to get to her as soon as possible. It could be a matter of life or death."

"Life or death? Goodness gracious, you're both so dramatic. Good that you found each other." She settled into her favorite chair and took a sip of coffee. "A cabin, you said. Can you describe it?"

"What do you mean describe it? How many c-c-can there be on your property?"

"There are all sorts of shacks around the farm, you know, here and there."

Rachel clarified that the one Tornado found was on the east side, next to the pumpkin patch, somewhere deep in the woods.

"Oh. He-he. You're probably talking about where Pa used to hang out. He called it his man cave. Quite a setup. I think he kept his hooch over there, too. I can't imagine why you think a nice young girl like Daisy would be in that old dump. I

61

don't believe anybody's been there since Pa met his maker."
She took another sip. "Are you sure I can't get anyone a cup?"

I interrupted. "Ma, we're kind of in a hurry. Can you give us directions?"

"Oh right, life or death. I forgot. Well, if it's the one I'm thinking of, it'll be real easy to find. Head on down to the edge of the old corn field. You can't miss a big Tree of Heaven at the north end. Go past it a little bit and turn left. Or, turn right if you're coming from the other side. Anyway, you'll see the path by a bunch of pawpaw trees. Follow it north, I think, and you'll run into a wood fence post. Turn there, and the path will take you right to it."

I thanked her, though it was next to impossible to memorize her kooky directions. I asked her to keep an eye out for Tornado as well. We'd become good friends, and I was concerned about her.

"Yes, I will. Tornado was a good woman."

"Clear as mud, right?" Rachel asked, when we left the house. "If she hasn't been up there in years, the paths she described will be completely overgrown. But we do have one piece of good luck. I can recognize a Tree of Heaven. Not sure about the pawpaw, though."

We mistook the pumpkin field for the old corn field Ma referenced, and; therefore, we never came upon the famous Tree of Heaven. And why we missed the pawpaw trees, which we wouldn't have recognized anyway, and why the wooden fence post we ran across was the wrong one.

Ma's directions were useless, and before we got completely lost, we decided to forget what she told us and head straight for the woods.

The fields we needed to cross had been ignored and allowed to grow out of control and, almost immediately our forward journey was reduced to a crawl as we plugged along, helping each other navigate the low branches of gnarled trees and the prickly and impenetrable Barberry bushes that grew everywhere.

"I wonder if we even need to go any farther in this direction," Rachel said, passing her backpack to me so she could squeeze through a narrow opening. "I can't believe Daisy could have made it through here on her own."

"Oh, yes she could." I lifted her pack up and went through. "Boy, this is heavy. What do you have in here?"

"Oh, sorry. Lots of stuff. You can never be too prepared."

"Damn! What the hell?"

"I said I was sorry the bag is so heavy. Set it down and I'll take it as soon as I get out of this mess."

"I'm not talking about your backpack. I just got snagged on this barbed wire. Tornado was right. It hurts like hell."

Rachel froze. The dilapidated wire fence was camouflaged by the bushes, and she was inches away from running into it herself. When we let our eyes focus, we saw that it twisted around in several directions.

"If this is the fence T-T-Tornado mentioned, maybe we're close to the cabin after all," I said. "See how old it is? Trees have grown right through it."

"And rusty. Glad I got my tetanus shot." Rachel tugged down another section of wire, so I could step over.

"Wish I had gotten one. All I know is that barbed wire usually means k-k-keep out," I said. "I wonder why they put it here?"

"I think we're about to find out."

As we dragged ourselves out of the brambles, we could make out the slumped down roof and crumbled chimney of an old shack.

We didn't see the guard dog, but we didn't want to take any chances, so Rachel tossed a stone on the roof to attract attention. When there wasn't a reaction, she threw another, and the loud noise it made rattling down the roof and dropping on the porch still didn't elicit a response.

"I don't know what we're going to find in there, but I doubt it's going to be pretty," Rachel said. "Are you sure you're ready?"

"I am, if y-y-you are," I replied, as we climbed the rotted steps. A padlock dangled open on the door hasp.

"Gosh, after going to the trouble of putting up all that barbed wire, you'd think they'd remember to lock up."

I grabbed the handle and gave it a tug, but the warped old door wouldn't give. Then I planted a foot against the frame for leverage and used both hands. This time I put my whole weight into the effort and the door swung open.

"Daisy?"

Other than a few rodents scurrying to the safety of cracks in the walls when sunlight hit the floor, there didn't appear to be any sign of life inside. Old pillowcases were tacked over the windows, and whiskey bottles lined their sills. In the corner was a cot that sagged dramatically in the middle. A sleeping bag lay smoothed out, and a fluffy pillow was neatly placed at the head. Atop a crate that served as a bedside table sat a sealed jar of Peter's Pickles and a half-full, clear, glass bottle with a cork. Rachel took a sniff and determined it was moonshine.

"It's Pa's hideaway all right," I said, admiring the girly pin up calendars from the last century tacked to one wall. Pork rinds spilled from an opened bag on a table. "Rats wouldn't leave chips for long. What do you make of it?"

"Hard to tell. The place stinks like mildew and something else I can't identify, but someone must be living here."

"I smell mothballs," I said, though that wasn't the other scent she was talking about.

"I don't know. It's not as bad as I expected," she said.

"It's worse for me. I was expecting to find Daisy."

9

There was a blanket heaped on the middle of the floor, and when I tossed it to the side a huge dust cloud filled the room. I was sorry the moment I flung it because Rachel reacted with a violent cough. I apologized and was desperate to do something, but she waved me away and regained her normal breathing on her own.

"Don't freak out. It's only the dust."

She was right. I had overreacted, because her coughing jag reminded me of a dramatic incident with Daisy that occurred on the third day of hiking together. I remembered it vividly, because it was the first time I'd witnessed anyone suffering from a serious asthma attack.

We'd been climbing a steep uphill grade for a while, when I remarked that she hadn't been very talkative. She didn't answer me, and before I could make a joke about how the peace and quiet was enjoyable, I heard her wheezing. I turned around to see Daisy crouched on the ground. Her face was blue, and she pounded on her chest as she struggled to breathe.

I'll never forget her panicked eyes when I rushed to her side. She could no longer speak, but she managed to point to her pack. Frantic, I dumped everything on the ground, hoping it would be easier to see what she wanted me to retrieve.

It took me a few minutes to realize what she needed was an inhaler. I almost missed it because she kept it in a little knit pouch. It was bright blue with a white daisy stitched to one side and a duck on the other, and I would never have bothered to look inside had she not pointed.

A few pumps later, she was breathing normally again. We sat leaning against each other as she recovered her strength, and I regained my calm. I'd saved her life and, as I gently stroked her hair, she repeated how grateful she was. I never thought of those actions as heroic, but rather as being lucky— lucky to turn around when I did, and lucky enough to locate the inhaler in the nick of time.

"I guess this is what they call irony," she said. "It was the last place you thought to look, but I keep it in that bag, so I can put my hands on it right away."

Rachel brought my mind back to the job at hand. She pointed to the back door and offered a suggestion. "Why don't I finish here, and you see what's back there? You can take my flashlight."

"Nah. You need it. I'll check the rest of the place and come back if I find anything interesting."

I stepped out into a small three-walled storage room and found a huge pile of backpacks, and when I pawed through a couple, I discovered they were still full of hiking supplies. Just then, Rachel shouted from the main room to say she'd found something. I told her she'd want to see what I found, first.

"Good grief!" she exclaimed, as she saw me rifling through the stack. "At least this clears up the mystery of the mildew."

There was a dozen or so packs in various stages of wear and tear. Canteens were still hooked to some of them, and rats had chewed through ones that once contained food. A collection of tarps and tents lay next to the backpacks, but I was discouraged that neither mine nor Daisy's were among them.

"I wonder whose stuff this is?" she asked. "Looks like Ma's Lost and Found."

"Can't be. She told me the farm didn't have one. Still, there's an awful lot of equipment here. People forget to take little things, but how could so many hikers f-f-forget their backpack?"

"I know. One more thing that doesn't make sense."

As she aimed her light, I started pulling things out of the pack on the top of the pile. We found tons of canned food, a few stocking caps, and at least one flashlight in every bag, one of which I commandeered right away. She shined the beam on a red bag I recognized belonging to the Australian. It was covered with colorful sewn-on patches from parks all over the world, and I wondered what it was doing here in the cabin. I realized I hadn't seen him since the day I left to buy the ring.

"He was supposed to be here when I came back," I said. "But he's gone, too, and I never got to give him this keychain I bought while I was in Harpers Ferry." I reached into my pocket and pulled out the half-keychain. The kangaroo was creepy looking in the dimly lit room.

Rachel sounded nervous. "Um, Strider? Check this out." She pulled off the keychain attached to the pack and held it up to her flashlight. It was one half of a kangaroo. When she put the half I purchased against the one she held, they snapped together perfectly.

"So, are we supposed to believe that he left the farm, went to Harpers Ferry, sold half of his k-k-keychain to the curio shop, and continued on his hike without a backpack?"

"Maybe. Ma said she paid him a lot of money, and the bag is pretty worn out. Maybe he didn't want it anymore."

"Are you kidding? We talked quite a while, and I knew he was proud of all the places he'd visited. Like this one." I fingered the Kalalau Trail patch. "This trail runs along the NaPali Coast on the island of Kauai, and he said it was the most spectacular stretch he'd ever hiked."

We put that mystery aside and once again rifled through the other packs. With two working flashlights, we each took half and make quick work of the pile.

Rachel found a set of keys. "Woah."

"What do you have?"

"A wallet. No money, but I found an ID."

The printing was faded on the driver's license, but when she held it against the light, she made out the name.

"Danielle. Danielle Houdeshell. Ring any bells?"

The name meant nothing, and I kept sorting through the bags. While the backpacks were full, we didn't find any surprises or patterns. A few contained Appalachian Trail Passports, and by their stamps, hikers seemed to be hiking both north and south.

"Looks more like s-s-stolen goods to me."

"Let's not jump to that conclusion. I mean, since everything is still basically untouched, why would you think they were stolen? No, I still say we stumbled on the farm's Lost and Found department."

I couldn't buy into her argument. We found plenty of IDs, but we didn't run across any money, so the thief was likely only interested in the cash. But that still didn't account for so many hikers forgetting their backpacks, considering it was all they owned. So, for me, it raised a larger question. Did the hikers ever leave?

I needed more clues, so I started over. This time we were more systematic, and we pulled out everything from each bag. Rachel worked fast, and before long she made a connection.

"Bingo!" she said, holding up a bloody sweatshirt.

I didn't get the significance.

"You may not recognize this, but I do. It's Tornado's. She used this to wipe off her blood from the barbed wire cuts she got last night."

We used both flashlights to examine the bloody shirt that Rachel swore she remembered seeing Tornado wearing. Even the size was right, and the blood was still damp. The fact that it was hers made things more alarming. Now, we found two backpacks belonging to two hikers that we'd been told had left the farm.

"But what about Daisy? Where's her stuff? And where's mine, for that matter?"

We were still digging around when someone clomped up the steps to the front porch. We shut off our flashlights and froze in place, not daring to make a sound. The boots stomped around inside and then stopped. For several minutes we heard nothing, and Rachel and I clung motionless, fearing the slightest movement might cause the floorboards to creak.

We stared at the back door for what seemed an eternity, but I counted out the minutes in my head and knew it had only been three. I'd been holding my flashlight up to use as a club the whole time, and my arm was getting tired. When I lowered it to rest, shifting my weight was enough for the floor to make a tiny creak.

The person inside started to pace again, and this time we could tell he was coming in our direction. When he stopped, the only thing separating him from us was the door. We raised our flashlights and were ready to clobber anyone who walked through.

But the door never opened, and, after standing in silence for what seemed an eternity, we thought we heard the intruder walk back and out the front door. We were still facing the back door, when we watched the metal latch rise and the doorknob turn. We held each other tighter.

The door flung open, and a light blinded us.

"Who's there?" It was a man's voice.

Clunk. We smashed his head with our flashlights.

"Hey, hey. Ow! Settle down. It's just me," Sparky said, illuminating his face. His eyes grew wide when he saw we were in an embrace. "Say, I didn't know you two were a thing."

Rachel was breathing heavily, but the first thing she blurted out was that we weren't a couple. I tried to find the words to make it plain that she was only helping me track down Daisy, my real girlfriend.

"Oh, uh huh. I see. Well, it looked a little lovey-dovey to me."

I accused him of scaring the crap out of us, but he said he'd seen beams of light crisscrossing through the window and wanted to check it out. Since the door to the shack was wide open, he walked in.

"I wonder what they use this place for?" He shined his light behind me. "And what's all this stuff? Is it yours?"

Rachel was quick to respond. "Are you nuts? Of course not. Did you think we brought it out here in your wheelbarrow?"

We filled him in on what we'd found and asked if he had a theory about how the stuff ended up there. He claimed he'd never been there before, though he seemed sure it was the one Tornado told him about.

He picked up a plastic soap container I had pulled from one of the backpacks. "Hey, I could use one of these. Do you suppose anybody would mind if I borrowed it?"

Rachel stepped in. "Sparky, do you think Ma knows about this place?"

He stopped rummaging for a minute. "Are you kidding? If it's on her farm, of course she does. Say, I could use another toothbrush, too. I wonder what else I can find."

While he picked through the belongings, I picked his brain about the Australian.

"Yep, he was on pumpkin duty a whole week. Complained all the time, but Ma paid him a fortune. I saw her hand it to him. Didn't he leave?"

"We thought so," Rachel said, holding up his red backpack. "And Tornado supposedly left, but her stuff is here, too. What do you make of that?"

"I dunno. Ma paid them both a lot of money. Maybe they got new stuff."

"Told you!" she said.

"Found one!" Sparky held a bright orange toothbrush.

"Sparky, I've been meaning to ask. Where's your t-t-tent? You aren't camping with the rest of us."

"Oh, Ma let me pitch mine near the compost pile. It's a bit far from the latrine, but it's quiet, and I've always liked the quiet. I'm the strong silent type. Well, I'll be off and let you two get back to whatever you said you were doing." He winked and left.

When he was out of sight we collapsed on the steps, wondering what had transpired. Going through other people's stuff was giving me the creeps, and we still hadn't made any progress finding Daisy. Rachel pulled my head onto her lap. She admitted something was definitely not right and promised not to leave my side until we figured it out. Then she gave my hand a squeeze.

"You know, I want to find her as much as you do."

I appreciated the sentiment, but I doubted her sincerity. After we rested a couple of minutes, I asked her to show me what she found in the main room. She aimed her flashlight while I felt under the cot. I had to stretch out flat on the floor, to reach all the way under and grab it.

"Holy shit! It's m-m-my backpack!"

"Whoopee! What a relief!"

"Yeah, but what the hell is it d-d-doing here?" I dumped everything out and spread it over the bed. "At least nobody stole anything. Everything is here."

"If nothing is missing, why do you keep saying someone is stealing things? You were gone, and maybe somebody turned it in."

"Come on. Don't you think it's weird that every time a hiker supposedly leaves, their gear ends up out here in this p-p-place?"

"Yeah, but if your theory's right, Daisy's backpack should be here, too."

I hated to admit to her point. Plus, it added to the mystery. By now I had a raging headache. The mildew was doing a number on me but, thankfully, I had my backpack and my bottle of aspirin. As I popped a couple in my mouth, Rachel mentioned running across quite a few prescription drugs.

"I pity the poor people who left all that medication behind. I know what it's like."

"You, too?" I said. "Daisy carries an inhaler with her. She said going anywhere without one would be a d-d-death sentence."

"An inhaler?" Rachel grabbed a pack she'd just examined. "Did it look something like this?"

She dangled a little blue bag, and the daisy on the side made my heart sink.

"Why didn't you tell me you found D-D-Daisy's backpack?"

"How was I supposed to know it was hers? I found the inhaler in the one belonging to Danielle Houdeshell."

Danielle. So that was Daisy's real name. Holding the little blue bag brought tears to my eyes.

"Just because we found her backpack doesn't mean s-s-something terrible has happened to her, does it?"

PART TWO

10

If Sparky was right, Ma had to be complicit in the disappearance of the hikers, too. When we left the cabin, I was steaming mad, and I wanted some answers. We noticed Sparky left by a different way, and we figured he knew something we didn't, so we took the same direction. Even if his route was difficult, any way out would be easier than the way in.

Our hopes were dashed when his path quickly faded away, and we found ourselves once again in a dense thicket. It was hot, and lugging two additional heavy backpacks and tents made the trip back every bit as treacherous and arduous as our way in.

Every time I had to step over or duck under a piece of barbed wire, I got more agitated, and, by the time we got to the farmhouse, I was in a rage. I banged on the kitchen door.

"Ma, we need to talk! And I better like what you have to say. Otherwise, I'm calling the police!"

"What? Back so soon?"

Ma was dressed like a gypsy. Around her neck hung multiple necklaces in various styles and metals, and the dozen or so bracelets on each wrist clattered when she pulled open the door. There was a ring on every finger and both thumbs. Some of them were set with gemstones and were quite lovely and contrasted with others that resembled plastic prizes from a gumball machine. The tinkling tune of a music box floating from inside the kitchen completed the picture.

"Come in. Come in. What's the matter now?"

I pulled Rachel in behind me, and we stood awkwardly as Ma went back to her seat at the kitchen table, where she was sorting through a small stack of watches. Next to her sat an old multi-tiered, turquoise, leatherette jewelry box. The top tray was filled with earrings, and strands of beads spilled out of the bottom drawer. A tiny ballerina spun at the top, the source of the music. Ma picked up one piece and fondled it under the bare bulb that hung over the table.

"What's all that?" I blurted. "More th-th-things you stole?"

"I beg your pardon?"

"Don't act innocent! Rachel and I found that cabin of yours, no thanks to your terrible d-d-directions. You've been lying to us!"

"*Us*? You and Rachel? Hmm. Do tell."

"We found all the stuff you've been stealing from the hikers, and we found evidence that someone is living there."

She didn't look up.

"Are we talking about the same place? The one with girly stuff on the walls?"

"Yes, and what difference does that make?"

"Because you called it '*my* cabin.' It was Pa's, not mine. I thought we went over that."

"His, yours. What's the d-d-difference?" I let my bag drop on the table with a thud, and she still didn't make eye contact with me. "But this is mine. I found it there. What do you have to say about that?"

"Well, I'd say you're one lucky guy. You've been looking for it long enough."

I showed her Daisy's backpack and told her we found the Australian's and Tornado's backpacks, too. I banged my fist on the table and insisted she clear up how they got there, and what happened to the hikers. To my astonishment, she ignored me. It was Rachel's condition that alarmed her more.

"Goodness me, you're all scratched up. Let me get you some salve."

Rachel shook her head. "We had to go through a lot of barbed wire."

"You must not have gone the way I said. Ain't no barbed wire that way." Before she limped over to find the ointment, she cracked open a jar of pickles. "Hungry?"

I couldn't believe her nonchalance. As I was about to bring her back to my question, a toilet flushed in a side room. The door to the small bathroom swung open, and I was taken off guard when the owner of the curio shop emerged. He was still drying his hands and no doubt as surprised to see us as we were to see him.

"Oh, sorry. Did I interrupt something?"

"Not at all, Peter. I was trying to convince these young people to try my pickles."

"Who on earth could refuse a Peter's Pickle? Say, that reminds me, I hope you have plenty. I wanted to pick up a jar while I'm here."

Ma giggled. "I already set some aside for you."

He turned to me. "Ah, the young man from my shop yesterday. What a coincidence."

"So, you know each other?"

In spite of the lengthy transaction that spanned two days, we had not introduced ourselves, but now I learned his name was Peter.

"But you don't look like Daisy," he said, extending his hand.

"Daisy? Of course not. I'm Rachel, but people mix us up all the time."

Ma raised her eyebrows. "They do?"

"And are you the Peter of pickle fame?" Rachel asked.

"No, no. A completely different person, but just the same, they're quite delicious. You can definitely taste it when someone puts body and soul into their work, like Missus Winter and the hikers do. Now, where were we?"

"I was about to show you Sally's brooch, when those two barged in."

"Oh, yes. Aunt Sally." He patted her hand. "I was so sorry to hear she passed."

She returned the pat. "Yes, we've all been grieving so. You know, I almost buried the brooch with her, but at the last minute, I found the note where she promised it to me."

"Wait a m-m-minute!" I exclaimed. "This is your jewelry?"

Peter was miffed. "Of course. I've been buying pieces from her family estate for years. In fact, the ring you purchased for your fiancée was part of her collection."

Ma beamed. "Which ring was that, Peter?"

"That delicate silver one encircled with the elaborate vines, remember? The inscription was to Dillon and Pat."

"Oh yes. What a coincidence! When they left us, I didn't remove it from my finger for months. It was one of my favorites, and I remember you practically begged me to sell it."

"Yes, and it was awkward being so persistent. Considering how tragically they died on their wedding night, I'm afraid I was a bit insensitive."

"Nonsense. I'm sure they would be thrilled that their ring was bringing such happiness to another couple." She gave us a snide glance.

"Okay, so the j-j-jewelry is yours, but what about all the stuff we found?"

"What is he talking about, Mrs. Winter?"

Ma caught Peter up on what had transpired when he was using the bathroom. "They accused me of stealing a few things they said they found over in Pa's man cave. You remember that old shack? He used to love that place, God rest his soul."

Ma crossed herself.

"I can't imagine that Mrs. Winter would steal anything."

"Well, maybe she didn't," said Rachel. "But somebody did. Hikers wouldn't leave stuff like that behind."

Ma sneered. "Goes to show what you know. You'd be shocked what people leave behind when they have a little money in their pockets. Seems hikers always gotta have the newest gadgets and *what's its* and *who's its,* even when they've got perfectly good stuff already."

"So, what is that pile then, your Lost and Found?"

"Lost and Found?" Ma's eyes brightened. "Yes. Yes, Rachel. That's exactly what it is. Been trying to explain that all day."

"Even if we were to believe that cabin is your L-L-Lost and Found, why would my backpack be there? I was only gone overnight."

"Well, how was I supposed to know whose it was? Somebody told me it was just left lying around after the owner of it left."

"And Daisy's, t-t-too?"

"There we go with Daisy again. Are we still talking about the same Daisy I engraved on your ring?"

"Yes. And when I got back from your shop yesterday, she wasn't here. Her tent, my stuff, everything was gone. I've been trying to find her ever s-s-since. Something very strange is going on around here."

"But you got your stuff back," said Ma. "And hers. Let's not forget that."

"Since there isn't an emergency, perhaps you could let Mrs. Winter and me get back to the work?" Peter lifted a locket from Ma's basket. "How much would it take for you to part with this little beauty?"

I grabbed it out of Peter's hand. "Wait a minute. This l-l-locket is exactly like the one you gave the Australian."

"It better be," she snorted, gently taking it back from me. "My grandfather gave my sister and me matching lockets, when we turned sixteen."

"Stop changing the subject. Rachel and I w-w-want you to tell us what happened to the hikers whose stuff we found, and you can start with Daisy."

Ma took a deep breath. "I'm not the one who changed the subject. You're the one obsessed with my locket. Listen, I've been trying to tell you something, young man, and I guess I'm just gonna have to come right out and say it."

She put a hand on my shoulder. "Think about it. Man lies to his old lady about where he's going. Stays out all night. She's got to wonder why."

I swallowed hard, afraid of what she would say next. She sat back in her chair.

"Maybe she thought you ditched her. I have a feeling Daisy wanted to get away from all this and you. You're going to have to face facts. You've been jilted."

"But, I found her inhaler. She would never leave without it."

"She could pick up another one in town."

"I was g-g-going to propose."

"It stings, I understand."

I was grasping for straws. "B-B-But she loved me."

Peter seemed sympathetic. "Strider, people get dumped all the time, isn't that right, Misses Winter?"

"Oh, Glory, yes!" she said with a chuckle.

I appreciated their candor, and I was embarrassed for the ugly accusations I hurled at her. "M-M-Ma, it seems I owe you an apology."

She turned upbeat. "Let's just forget about it. I'm guessing you two are hungry. What y'all need is some of this hot dish I'm making for Peter. Hope you like eggplant. It'll be ready soon."

"I hope it's Emma's Eggplant."

"The one. The only."

I was feeling foolish but thankful that I'd been saved from the embarrassment of calling the police. "I don't suppose you'd b-b-buy the ring back, would you?"

Peter apologized and said it would be out of the question. He'd never be able to buff out the names and engrave new ones now, the silver would be too thin. "Of course, then we also have that dreadful affair of passing on bad luck, were I to sell the ring to an unsuspecting couple *as is.*"

He reached over and pulled back the cuff of my shirt. "Do you mind? Oh, very nice," he said, admiring my watch. "I'd be happy to buy that from you, though."

"No thanks." As they left the kitchen, I muttered, "Oh yeah, that 'dreadful affair.' I should have taken my chances on the bad luck."

Rachel took my arm. "Well, I'm here to help you turn that bad luck around."

Maybe Ma was right, and it was time for me to face the fact that Daisy left me. But I realized Ma managed to get us out without accounting for the missing hikers. Her story about the Lost and Found didn't add up, either, because earlier she told me the farm didn't even have one.

"And I don't understand how she could she get all that stuff over there with that bum leg of hers," Rachel said.

My gut instinct told me to leave, but I decided to stick around a little longer to unravel some of the mystery.

Rachel suggested I take a rest since I'd been going full out for two days. "I'll go back to the kitchen," she said. "I need to clock some hours. Someone needs to finance our hike."

I tactfully ignored her suggestion that we comingle our cash. It was a beautiful day with a slight wind. When I checked in with Red, he was working in the garden and already sweating buckets. I couldn't tell whether he was pleased to have me back or not.

"Did you ever find Dani?" he grumbled.

"Who?"

"Danielle, your girlfriend. Goes by Daisy, sometimes Daisy Duck."

"What the hell? I just found out her n-n-name myself. How come you know it?"

"She told me. How else? That's why I wasn't sure who you meant yesterday when you asked me if I'd seen Daisy. I only knew her as Dani."

God, I was such an idiot. I even had the ring engraved *Strider and Daisy*. It didn't occur to me that Daisy wasn't her real name, not that Strider was mine. I sighed. "Well, it doesn't matter, I'm never going to find her, because now I realize what everyone else figured out. She d-d-ditched me."

Red shrugged. "Happens to the best of us."

I stared at the configuration of raised beds. There were ten rows of five beds each. "Boy, you got a lot done. I was supposed to fill in that one over there, but you must have gotten to it before me."

"I didn't do it. It was like that when I started this morning."

I picked up a spade and started a new one. We worked in silence for a while and didn't take breaks, except for water. He was standing on the bottom of a bed he'd dug when he broke the silence. "So, what are you going to do?"

"I'll stick around and work a while, I guess. I've still got two more weeks before my new job starts, and I need to make some money. At least the two hundred b-b-bucks I spent on that ring." I also wanted to figure out what the hell was going on, but I wasn't about to reveal my plans.

"Yeah, not a bad idea. And it'll probably help take your mind off things."

"Hope so. Call me c-c-crazy, but part of me still thinks she'll come back."

"Speaking of crazy, I see you've been spending a lot of time with Rachel."

"Crazy? What's that supposed to mean? She's been a real godsend. I couldn't have made it through all this without her."

"Oh, she's a charmer all right."

"Yeah, but you said 'crazy.' What do you mean?"

"Never mind. Forget what I said."

"Come on. By now I can take anything."

"I'd just be careful if I were you."

"Care to elaborate?"

"No. I'll leave it at that."

Daisy

When the key turned and released the ancient tumblers, the old door lock clanked free. Daisy was still wearing the hood someone put over her head and couldn't see who entered, but the rattling of dishes on a tray told her at least food was on the way.

"I thought you'd forgotten me," she uttered when her gag was removed.

"I tried to," the voice said matter-of-factly. "I hope I don't have to remind you about keeping your voice down. Phew! Now see, you made a mess again!"

"I couldn't help it. You kept me tied to this chair all day."

"Shut up! Here's a towel and some shorts. Clean yourself up, and hurry. I don't have all day to fuss over you."

While it was a great relief to have the ropes removed from her wrists and ankles, the hood remained secured, and without the benefit of sight Daisy did her best to wipe herself off and change into the baggy pair of hiking shorts thrown in her lap.

"Did you bring food? I'm starving."

"Listen, you'll find a table directly in front of you, and that's where the tray is. You've got three minutes to eat."

"Can I have something to drink?"

"What? Do you think I'm some sort of monster? If you'd stop talking, you'd find a glass of water on the tray, right in front of you."

As promised, in three minutes, the tray was pulled back, and Daisy was bound to her chair again.

"How long are you planning to keep me here?"

"As long as it takes."

"What's that supposed to mean?"

The response to her question was to get her gag replaced. The door closed quietly, and Daisy heard the lock go clunk.

11

To get things sorted out in their heads some people take long walks or meditate. Hard physical exertion suited me best. And I had plenty to figure out, so doing some heavy lifting in the garden was exactly what I needed.

I'd always thought of myself as level headed, and my life as normal and generally uneventful, but since I started on the trail things were topsy-turvy. I began to question my judgment and recent choices I made.

I had already leased a new apartment but maxing out my credit cards to set it up was something I'd never done before. My new position was a huge promotion and gave me a big bump in pay, so I wasn't concerned about the short-term debt.

Buying the damned ring was uncharacteristically impulsive, and I blamed my new troubles on it. It wasn't even my idea. I compounded the problem by falling for the superstition about the engraving. Instead of staving off bad luck, that stupid decision cost me my girlfriend.

It frightened me how quickly I had evolved from being a single man in an unfamiliar setting to being practically engaged overnight. Daisy pushed the commitment, but I couldn't pin all the blame on her. I'd been complicit and reckless. But I did love her, and I wasn't ready to chalk up my infatuation as merely sexual. I distinctly remembered the romance and falling in love. And it being reciprocal.

Maybe it wasn't the ring's fault. I hadn't been particularly superstitious before now, but I toyed with the idea that the shop itself might be the culprit. That a sinister force enticed us to window shop, and then another more powerful one lured us in, where we fell victim to the recommendation for work that sent us to the farm.

I knew *juju* wasn't a very good reason, but if I was going to figure out what happened to the others, I had to start acting smarter, beginning with Rachel. Her flirting had not gone unnoticed, and, even though I acknowledged a budding mutual attraction, I wasn't eager to make the same mistake and jump into a relationship with her or anyone else.

Until she put her hand on my shoulder, I didn't realize she had crept beside me, and I recoiled from her touch.

"Hey, slow down, babe! You're working too hard, which is why I'm here. Listen, I just finished an interesting conversation in the kitchen."

At that moment, I saw Ma strolling not far from where we'd stood, and she gave us a friendly wave.

"She's worried about us."

"Us?"

"Yeah, she said we're the hardest working hikers she can remember, and she hopes we'll stay for a long time. She also said that under the circumstances and due to all our stress, she's giving us the rest of the day off with pay! She went all out and made this picnic for us. Turns out there's more than the eggplant dish." Rachel held up a basket.

I ignored her use of "us" and "we."

"She thought we'd enjoy the pool."

"This place has a pool? You've got to be k-k-kidding."

Rachel shrugged. "She gave me directions. What do you think? Want to go?"

I considered the shovel in my hands and my sweat-soaked shirt. Her wild hair and glimmering eyes stared hopefully at me, and the picnic basket loaded with farm fresh goodies looked promising.

"I'm in," I said. "Especially if the directions to the pool are better than the ones to the cabin."

Following them this time was a snap, and we wandered to a part of the farm I had not yet explored. Like the way to everything else on the farm, the way to the pool was not without its twists and turns, but judging by the well-worn path, it was obviously popular. Why had no one ever mentioned it before?

I took the lead and Rachel called out directions from a yard or two behind. As I emerged from the scraggly brush, I stopped abruptly and laughed out loud.

"What's so funny? Isn't there a pool?"

"Oh, yeah. And it's p-p-picture perfect!"

The small pond must have been the family swimming hole, back when there was a family. The water was relatively clear, and the grass lawn around it had been mown. While the deck was rickety, I guessed it was safe enough to walk on. A narrow diving board extended from the end.

Even with a few missing slats, the three handmade, Adirondack-style lounge chairs were inviting and a sharp contrast to the foreboding electric fence that provided the backdrop.

Rachel dropped her things and spread out the blanket Ma had sent with her. When she plopped the basket on the picnic table, the noise disturbed the tranquility beneath it, and three long, black snakes slithered out, their tongues flicking at Rachel's feet on their way to the water.

"Eek! Did you see that?"

"Yeah, ha-ha. They're probably just water snakes. They're not going to bother anybody."

"But there were three! And they weren't afraid of me." Putting aside her fear of the snakes, she unloaded the homemade bread, jams, and the eggplant hot dish. There was even a small jar of pickled ramps. "Hungry?"

"Not yet," I lied, hearing my stomach rumble. I wanted to eat but the pond was too inviting. I was tempted to skinny dip, but as I stripped off my shirt and pants it occurred to me that Rachel might get the wrong impression, so I didn't remove my boxers.

I ran down the length of the dock and leaped into the air, crashing into the cold blackness with a pounding cannonball. The pond was deeper than I imagined, and when my feet at last touched the bottom, I jetted back to the surface, spraying water into the air like a fountain.

"Woof! Come on in, the w-w-water's fine!"

I was doing the backstroke in the widest part of the pond, when Rachel raced down the dock, and I caught a flash of skin which confirmed that she was wearing only her underwear and t-shirt.

"Ooh, ick!" she squirmed when her feet touched the bottom. "It's slimy and sticky."

I swam back to join her at the shallow end. "Most lakes and ponds have mucky bottoms," I explained as a turtle swam by. I was about to touch its head when she shouted a warning.

"Don't!"

The turtle had creaked open its jaw to show off its razor-sharp jagged beak, and I pulled back before it could tear my finger to shreds.

"I could tell it was a snapping turtle by the big head," she said. "You're lucky. I once saw one bite a guy's finger clean off."

She splashed me first, and then I splashed back. Before long, the fun turned into an epic water battle. Rachel admitted she couldn't swim, so, in deference to her, we stayed close to the edge where it was shallow. Still, it was deep enough for me to sneak up on her underwater and pretend to nip like a turtle.

The horseplay continued into the afternoon, until we dragged ourselves back to the dock to dry off in the sun. I was exhausted and lay on my back and closed my eyes. Rachel curled up next to me. My stomach growled, and she teased me with a reminder of all the delicious things Ma had packed for our picnic.

"Sounds yummy. What a wonderful ending…to a horrible d-d-day!"

"Oh, honey. Let's not go there again." She traced her finger on my chest. "Maybe she got cold feet. I mean, you barely knew each other."

I didn't mind her touching me, and I made no move to pull away. "And that's just it. She was the one who kept pushing the engagement. To be honest, I was in no rush. In fact, I felt a little off about things becoming so serious."

"Who wouldn't? I'm sorry, and it's probably not my place to say, but the whole thing never made much sense to me. Marrying someone you've only known for two weeks? Makes me wonder…" she trailed off.

"Wonder what?"

"Well, if maybe she was hiding something else, besides her name."

Her comment stung, but it was fair. I had similar thoughts, and now I was starting to see things weren't adding up.

I decided to change the subject. "What about that p-p-picnic?"

Rachel's finger still danced on my chest. "Sure, in a minute, but listen, there's something else I've been meaning to tell you."

My eyes were closed, and I was enjoying the attention. "Should I be worried? I'm pretty relaxed right now."

"It's not that big a deal, really. I just wanted to talk a little about Red."

"What about him?"

"I'll get to the point. I'm not sure you should trust him."

Rachel began to spell out why. When she initially arrived at the farm, Ma asked Red to show her the ropes, but there was really nothing to it, and Rachel caught on right away. Even when it was obvious that she knew what she was doing, he continued to hang around to supervise. At first, she wasn't bothered.

"He asked if I was single, which wasn't *that* strange. I mean he wouldn't have been the first guy to make a pass at me."

She said that Red crept closer and asked increasingly more personal questions. Before long, he was close enough to touch her, and that was when things officially got creepy. In that low voice of his, he acknowledged how scary it must have been for a girl to camp by herself. That there could be any number of threats lurking in the woods. He urged her to stay in his tent with him.

"Of course, I told him I wouldn't. A woman knows a red flag when she sees one."

She backed away and told him to bug off. He got angry and accused her of thinking she was too good for him. When she called him a jerk, he sulked away after mumbling about having to get back to work.

"'It can be hard for a woman traveling by herself. You have to learn to be firm. You guys have been working together a lot, so I thought I should say something. I only hope he wasn't the reason Daisy freaked out and left. I mean, who knows what really happened between the two of them in his tent?' Then I couldn't hear him anymore."

I had finally gotten relaxed, and now Rachel's comments started to stress me out again. All three of my friends told me different versions of rather inconsequential events. Daisy and Rachel's opposite recollections of working in the kitchen with Ma, and Rachel and Red's warnings about each other. I was being lied to, and I didn't understand why. And I didn't understand why I had to choose who to believe.

Rachel had been my rock for the past couple of days, and I came to trust her; yet, I couldn't imagine Red doing the things she described. I decided to let things play out and learn whom I could trust. My stuff turned up missing once, and I had no intention of being the next missing hiker.

I tested the waters with Rachel. I wanted her as an ally, but I wasn't sure where she stood. "So, how did you feel about M-M-Ma's explanation?"

She rolled her eyes. "What do you mean, explanation? She didn't tell us anything we didn't already know."

It was comforting she agreed with me, and I looked forward to figuring things out with her. For now, though, her hands had moved to my shoulders, and I was loving the massage.

When she slipped her fingers under to rub my shoulder blades, her long strokes stopped, and I felt her poke around. "Hey, what's this thing?"

"Oh, that? I got that scar from an old ice-skating accident."

"I don't think I'm feeling a scar. Sit up for a minute."

I lifted my shoulders a little, and she screamed. "Yuck, what is that?"

I felt around to where she was pointing. "Oh, crap, a l-l-leech!" I said, peeling it off and flipping it into the water.

"Ew, that's disgusting," she said, wiping off the hand that touched it. "Sit up some more!"

Her squeal confirmed that my back was covered with them, and it took her a long time to screw up the courage to even touch one again, not to mention peel them off. Each time she picked at one, she gave another little scream. Then, I saw her panic on her face.

"W-W-What is it? What else is on me?"

"On you? My god. I wonder if any got on me?"

I tried to sound calm. "Only a couple," I lied, seeing a half a dozen on her back. "Don't f-f-freak out. I've got it."

While I peeled each one from her back, she checked the rest of her body, and when she discovered them on the insides of her thighs, her shriek could be heard for miles. She kicked her legs, which made it nearly impossible for me to remove them.

"Here is another one, hold still." That final leech was disgustingly fat, and it split open when I pulled on it, spilling blood all over her leg. It was gross, but I couldn't stop laughing at her reaction.

"What's so funny? Get me out of here!"

"I didn't expect you to be so squeamish. It's kind of c-c-cute."

"Squeamish? I'm terrified!"

I continued what I thought was a joke. "What about that p-p-picnic?"

"Are you kidding? Snakes, leeches, and snapping turtles. This place is creeping me out. We're going back."

As we stood to go, she pointed to one more leech attached at my belly button. By then, even I didn't think it was funny anymore. Rachel got a head start and dashed down the dock, and I watched her stop first at the picnic table, and then to the lounge chairs.

"What the hell is going on?" she cried. "Somebody stole our clothes!"

12

I should have pitched my tent the moment I brought my gear back from the cabin. Now, because I was only wearing underpants, I wanted to set it up quickly, and I was grateful for all the shortcuts and tips Daisy showed me. At least the threatening skies hadn't manifested into rain. Rachel offered to let me stay with her again, but I put her off. That night, I would be tenting solo.

Waking the next morning physically refreshed reminded me of the joys of going to bed early. One look to the side and my mood turned sour. Instead of Daisy's warm and inviting body in the space next to me, now only sat her backpack, and I thought of those mornings not so long ago when we followed our morning sex with a communal shower.

It was a sobering thought that today would be the first real day I'd have to begin the process of moving on. My new life would start with a full day of work, the first of many I had planned. If everything went well, I would stay at least one more week, which would allow me to pay off my credit cards and start fresh. I'd even have a nice little cushion.

Working full out for seven days straight would be strenuous, but now that I could take a dip in the pond every day after work it sounded manageable. A leech or two wouldn't to be enough to keep me away.

Days before, Red and I ran an imaginary line down the middle of the garden, and we each took responsibility for half, so it was easy for me to begin where I left off. He had worked alone while I was away searching for Daisy, but without a little friendly rivalry, he slacked off and was behind, so I knew it would be easy to catch up. Working entire days again with him was going to be fun, but I wondered if Rachel's insights would color my feelings and keep me at arm's length.

Aside from a nod when we met that morning, we didn't speak. Instead, we got right to work, Red at his end and me at the other. For the first twenty or thirty minutes, I focused on getting my rhythm back and taking my frustrations out on the earth with my spade. There had been no rain for some time, only threats, and the ground was as hard as steel.

But I was naturally competitive and so was Red, and soon I found him matching my speed. Our eyes met more frequently, as we monitored each other's progress, and soon those side glances became grins, as our competition became more playful. When we stopped for water, I broke our verbal stalemate by apologizing for my earlier behavior in the confrontation about Daisy.

Red wiped sweat from his head with a dirty towel he kept tucked in his pants pocket and told me to forget about it.

"I would have done the same thing if it had been about my girlfriend." But then he laughed and asked me where I'd been. "You really stink."

When I told him about swimming with Rachel, he laughed again. He had been there once before and said it took him days to get rid of the pond scum smell.

"I guess you really liked her, huh? Dani, I mean."

I cringed. It was odd to hear him call her "Dani." "Yeah, I still do, even though she j-j-jilted me."

She was the first woman to find my stupid stutter sexy. It embarrassed me my whole life, which is probably why I became a programmer and spoke JavaScript all day. "I just haven't had much luck with women lately."

"With an ugly mug like that, I guess not."

"Really, Daisy was my first serious girlfriend in a long time, unless you count some anonymous flings I had online."

"You, too? I deleted all my dating apps before I started my hike."

It was embarrassing to admit I'd had more than a few. I told him about getting messages from women with profile pictures that were clearly stolen from the Internet, and how most of them wanted to roleplay or sext, neither of which interested me. I could only imagine who was at the other end of those messages, sitting at home all day plucking away at a computer.

In an effort to be more approachable, I changed my profile picture to a snapshot of a friend's dog excitedly licking my face, and, soon after, the novelty paid off. The sender's profile picture was different from the others. She was blowing out the candles of a birthday cake and looked like any real woman in her late twenties. The photo left a lot to the imagination, but from what I could see of her face, she was cute.

Her message was simple: "I like what I see. Want to connect?" Her handle was CutePuppy124.

We began with easy conversation, sharing our online horror stories, and I got a big laugh when she sent me screenshots of a lengthy argument she'd had with a man who had claimed in his texts to be Ryan Reynolds. We swapped many photos or at least I sent her several of me. She said her phone's camera wasn't up to the task, and it put me on the alert.

Still, she seemed genuine in every other way, and I gave her a pass on the lack of photos. Soon, our relationship advanced to the next important milestone: a phone call.

"Been there, done that," Red said, enjoying the story. By now we were both sitting on the ground and resting against the fence.

When the big day arrived, I couldn't wait, but my heart pounded from nerves. While I fully expected her to sound normal, I'd read enough stories about creepy Internet stalkers and men who faked being a woman online to be skeptical.

CutePuppy124 was none of that. She was light and bubbly like her name, and something about the timbre of her voice instantly put me at ease. Not surprisingly, conversation was a bit awkward at first, not helped by some chattering and giggling in the background, which I learned came from her sister and a friend, who were giving her grief for chatting with a guy she'd met online.

Against all odds, my romance with CutePuppy124 not only thrived, but the conversations became more substantive, and we started having catch-ups on the phone several times a week, paired with endless back and forth text messages. Soon, we couldn't get enough of each other. We'd been hinting at the possibility of meeting in person for weeks, and we agreed it was the right time. By now the stakes were high, and I was nervous.

But it never happened. We set many dates and convenient places to meet, but she always had a reason to cancel. The first excuse was a horrible cold, and I could tell she wasn't faking, because I could hear it in her voice.

The next few dates fell apart, too—one because of being required to stay late at her office, and the rest for other perfectly plausible reasons. Each time she sounded extremely upset and promised it wouldn't happen again. Until it did. That time the excuse was a flat tire, and she asked if I could come help her. By then, I'd had it. I didn't offer to help, and I balked at rescheduling. In fact, I shut down the whole relationship, grateful I never told her my real name.

"Meanwhile, I'd met someone else on the same site. I mean, what was I supposed to do? CuteP-P-Puppy124 was giving me the runaround."

"Uh, oh. I see where this is going," Red said.

The new one turned into phone sex almost immediately, and I chalked it up to the frustration that built up for the past month or so. It wasn't the kind of connection I wanted, and it didn't last long. I didn't even remember her name.

"While all this was going on, CutePuppy124 wouldn't stop texting and calling. She begged me to get back with her, insisting we were meant for each other."

I never responded, but I couldn't bear to block her, because I wasn't over her, either. Still, she was aware I was moving away.

Someone told me not to count on having reliable cell phone service in the mountains, so the day I left, I posted that I was taking a vacation from the app. *Appalachian Trail bound*, I wrote, adding a few notes about my itinerary. I couldn't imagine being without technology, but at least I'd be rid of women for a while.

"Or so I thought, until I met Daisy. The last few days were wild, and maybe it was just being on the r-r-rebound, but that's how it happened."

"Man, what you did was harsh," Red said. "I don't want to get all righteous, but rebounding or not, it was kind of a dick move to blow off CutePuppy124. I could never have ghosted her like that."

"Yeah, and I feel bad. So, what should I do?"

"If I were you, the next time I got a signal, I would call her and explain everything. Tell her you still have feelings for her, and you want to start over, in person." He shrugged. "But I'm hardly one to give advice."

Then he admitted to having worn the opposite shoes, where he played the CutePuppy124 role. In his case, though, the woman dropped him after the second time he didn't show up.

"She was right to break it off," Red said. "I learned a big lesson that day about respecting women."

I wondered how it was possible that the guy sitting next to me was the same lecher Rachel so vividly described. It was obvious he didn't have a creepy bone in his body. I was glad we talked and eager to take his advice and call CutePuppy124 as soon as my phone picked up a signal.

When Rachel stopped by, Red took it as his cue to leave.

"It's not you, Rachel," I joked. "I think he left because I smell like 'eau de p-p-pond scum.'"

"Apparently, we both smell like that awful pond because Ma told me I couldn't work with her until I washed up."

13

Tornado

When Tornado came back to the campfire the night before, she announced that she was exhausted, and if anyone wanted her help in the morning she'd need a wakeup call. She was badly cut from the barbed wire, though, and what she needed first was a shower. Sparky was all too familiar with cuts, and jumping at the chance to be helpful, he ran to the house to get Ma's old-fashioned salve. Tornado was drying off when he returned, and she was touched that the weird guy went to so much effort to bring her the little tin.

"You'll like it," he said, lifting up his shirt. "I use it on all my scratches, see?"

Tornado applied the salve immediately, not minding or caring that she'd have to endure his rambling. Everyone was used to it, and she tuned him out almost immediately.

"So, what do you say?" he asked. "Will you help me?"

"Uh, huh? I'm sorry, I was focusing on these cuts and wasn't paying attention. What do you want me to do?"

"I feel bad that I wasn't around to be part of the search party. I'm kind of a night owl, and I'd be happy to explore that cabin myself, if you'd show me where it was. I understand if you don't want to go the whole way, but maybe you could point me in the right direction."

She was not in the mood to go back so soon, but she felt guilty about not checking to see if Daisy was the cabin. Now, the combination of a nice shower and the generous amount of camphor in Ma's salve made Tornado refreshed and energized. Besides, the way Sparky framed the request, she wouldn't have to go the whole way, and it wouldn't take long.

Tornado led him across the pumpkin field, their way illuminated by silvery light from a strong moon, and the distant wailing of coyotes kept them company as they neared the hill leading up to the family cemetery.

"Damn those coyotes," Tornado said. "It sounds like they're right on top of us."

"Yeah, and I don't see how they got in with the fence and all. Maybe they chewed a hole through it somewhere."

Before she could acknowledge the ridiculous notion that a coyote could chew through an electric fence, a racket from the direction of the hill drew their eyes. The silhouette of the grave markers and cemetery fence was joined by another figure, which was moving. The howling grew louder, and Tornado assumed more animals had joined the pack, and she was afraid of being seen.

"Let's head for the woods over there on our left before they attack us. There ought to be a tall tree we can climb."

"Oh, I wouldn't worry about a couple of coyotes," he said, starting a lecture on the subject. "Even a single one can make a lot of noise, but they do it on purpose to make it sound like there's more of them. It's why they're called the 'song dog.' Oh, and they don't normally attack humans."

But Tornado didn't hear a word. Her adrenaline had kicked in, and she dashed off to the woods. As she pushed carelessly through a small thicket, a wicked prickly branch whipped across her face. It lacerated her skin and sent her glasses flying.

Behind her came a grow like the one she heard at the cabin, and while the sound momentarily paralyzed her, she was relieved it wasn't a coyote. From the sniffing and slobbering, she could tell the mongrel was only a few yards behind her.

Hot fangs clamped down on her leg, piercing the skin of her calf. But it could have been worse. Thanks to her blue jeans, the monster only tore away a mouthful of denim, and not a chunk of her flesh.

She jumped for the first tree that was easy to climb, and the rough bark punctured her palms and fingertips. Her muscles ached and strained, as she shimmied high enough to avoid the dog's teeth. Exhausted and scared, she straddled a large tree branch.

It was too dark to see where Sparky went, but she remembered hearing him run past her on the forest floor below. She didn't call out for fear of drawing attention, but, in spite of her silence, the dog found her tree. It sniffed and pawed at the trunk for a few minutes before it lost interest and skulked off.

She remained straddled on the branch for hours, long after the animal left, changing her position each time the discomfort became too severe. At last she found a crook large enough to settle in and lean back against, and soon she fell asleep.

What woke her was not a wild dog, but serious itching on her hands and arms. It had spread to her neck and face by the time she realized she was leaning against poison oak.

She needed to climb down, but with her uncorrected vision she couldn't see if the animal was nearby, and she cursed herself for losing her glasses. She was miserable and only wanted to get back to camp. "Sparky! Help me!"

Her call went unanswered. It wasn't until the afternoon that she felt it was safe enough to climb down. When she touched the ground, she only took a few steps before the hoot of an owl startled her, causing her to fall. Was it a warning?

She needed to find her way back to camp, but she was so twisted around and disoriented that she had no idea which direction to turn. After staggering aimlessly in a field for a while, she stumbled into a grassy patch next to a pond and lay down in a comfortable spot under a willow tree.

She felt her shoulders relax for the first time in hours and let out a big sigh at the tiny relief it provided. Tiny and short-lived.

Splashing and laughing woke her, and she recognized Strider's voice, though she couldn't identify the girl by hers. Was she Rachel or Daisy? Judging by the squealing and the laughter, she assumed it was Daisy and that they were whooping it up to celebrate their reunion. She was more convinced a little later, when after squinting, she could tell the two people were touching.

Tornado wanted to call for help, but her throat was raw, and the best she could manage was a tortuous whisper. She'd made the mistake of rubbing her eyes and the swelling reduced the openings to slits.

The rest of her was a mess, too. Her whole body itched, and angry pus oozed from the lesions on her enflamed cheeks. She imagined if anyone saw her crawling out of the bushes looking like that, they'd mistake her for a horror movie extra, so she decided to hang back and discretely follow them at a distance. Frustrated, she closed her eyes and drifted off.

An hour or so later, a *plop* of something that had leaped into the pond woke her up. It was followed by a slippery feeling, and, as she peered through slits in her eyes, a long, brown snake slithered over her forearm. Her heart froze when she recognized the markings. A copperhead. One bite could send her into deadly paralysis. Luckily, it was chasing whatever had jumped into the pond, and it wriggled past without acknowledging her.

She saw Strider and the girl running away from the pond. If she was going to follow them, she had to get moving. Backing out from her hiding place, she heard a twig snap behind her. Her heart thumped. *What is it this time?*

She didn't see anyone or anything, but she could no longer rely on her eyesight. Being in constant danger kept her on high alert and amplified every sound in the woods, so she didn't know if her hearing was reliable, either. There were so many places something creepy could hide, and camouflaged by the brush, they could be watching her even now.

Even with blurred vision, she could see it was a well-worn path, and she'd soon be back at camp. But then the unmistakable crunching sound of human footsteps alerted her. Someone was approaching slowly, possibly trying to sneak up on her. Who would be shadowing her? The tiny hairs at the base of her neck stood on end, and she bolted.

Pounding footsteps behind her confirmed she was being chased, and she soon realized it was a run for her life. The path abruptly ended at a corner of the fence, and she was trapped.

"Who are you?" she demanded. "What do you want?"

A figure stepped out of the trees. It wore a flour sack over its head as a disguise. Holes were cut for the eyes and mouth, but not one for the nose, distorting the hidden face. But while she couldn't identify the details of the assailant, she certainly recognized the rusty hand cultivator in its gloved hand.

"Leave me alone!" she cried. There was nowhere to go, and she panicked.

The figure took its time. Tornado's only escape was over the fence, and she hoped she'd be fast enough. She turned to climb, but she was too late.

Three sharp prongs clawed into her back, ripping her open from shoulder to tailbone. When the assailant pulled the cultivator free, she crumpled to the ground, landing on her mutilated back.

"Please," she begged in a weak voice. "Please stop." The cultivator struck again and again, this time into her belly. A hot bubble of blood trickled out of her swollen mouth.

During the repeated stabbings, the flour sack mask worked itself off.

"You." Tornado gargled around spurts of blood. "Why?"

The attacker quietly removed the weapon and wiped it clean but said nothing. Tornado was half-dead and out of energy, but she knew she wouldn't get another chance.

She swung a leg out, knocking across her attacker's legs, sending the assailant sprawling to the ground. Using the next split second to her advantage, Tornado wobbled to her feet and launched herself as high as she could. She grabbed the fence with both hands.

The shock hit her like a bolt of lightning.

Her screams lasted a full thirty seconds as the current pulsed through her body, crackling and melting her skin. When the fence was through with her, it gave off a low hum and a long buzzing, followed by a pop. Then it went silent.

14

I stripped down and entered the shower room, annoyed that someone left a toiletries kit on the only available shelf, leaving no room for my own. That small frustration was quickly forgotten, when I turned on the faucet and was more disappointed to find no running water. Rachel was waiting for me outside.

"What the hell? The sh-sh-shower's not working."

"The electricity is off, too. The kitchen was dark, and we had to work by candlelight."

I flipped the light switch, and when the lights didn't come back on, I knew what was wrong. "Looks like Ma blew a fuse. A real one, this time."

Most wells used an electric water pump, and I knew we wouldn't be able to use the shower again until we got the power back on, so I went to the house to see if I could help. Ma was on the porch when I got there.

"Happens all the time," she said. "Critters run into the fence and short the damn thing out. But, you're hikers. You should be used to not having electricity."

I thought it unlikely that one small animal could short out the whole system, but I ignored her explanation and offered to change the fuse.

"That would be nice, if I could only put my hands on them. They're around here somewhere." In the meantime, she suggested we use the pond if we wanted to wash up. Or, we didn't even need to go that far. There was an old hand pump on the way. Pa used to graze cattle out there, and she said it was still working.

"You walked right by it when you went to the pond. Anyway, you can't miss it."

Rachel was in a funk. She thought I'd given her a hard time when she freaked out over the leeches. I probably sent the wrong message, too, when I insisted on sleeping in separate tents. I was plain tired, but I didn't blame her for imagining our relationship was cooling. Besides, the lingering smell of pond scum was disgusting, and we were both feeling unsexy.

I made the mysterious and remote alternative water supply sound romantically primitive, and she perked up at the prospects of us standing naked together in the afternoon sun, one washing while the other pumped.

I'd had the whole day to think about my life and decided to take Red's advice. As soon as I found a signal, I'd call CutePuppy124 and try to start over with her.

But in the meantime, I'd see how things played out with Rachel. Life was short, and I was finally going to start living in the moment. As we headed for the pond, we bumped into Red, who was hot and dripping with sweat, as usual. He, too, was unhappy to have no running water.

He saw our towels. "Where are you guys going, the beach?"

I started to tell him about the hand pump, and Rachel stopped me with a kick to my shins. Red saw her reaction and knew what to say.

"Hey, have fun. I'm tired, and I think I'll go back to my tent. The power ought to be back on soon."

Ma was right. While tall weeds camouflaged it, the pump was where she claimed it would be. A mere two feet high, the rusty top stuck out of the ground through the rotting wooden platform made from an old pallet. Its handle resisted at first, but after putting some effort into it, I got it to move up and down.

"Do you think it's going to work?" she asked. "It doesn't sound good."

I was not discouraged, and it only took a few quick pumps for crystal clear water to gush out.

"Whoopee!"

This time neither of us held back, and we ripped off all our clothes. In seconds we stood before each other stark naked for the first time. After staring at each other for a few moments to satisfy our mutual curiosities, I reached for the pail.

"You can go f-f-first," I offered, filling it to the brim. I gently poured water over her head, watching it flow down her neck and shoulders. I used two buckets while she soaped up, and it took several more to rinse her off.

"That was just magnificent," she said, relieved to be fresh again. "Your turn."

We switched roles, and I took my time as well. The water was cold, but it felt good, and when I was finished, Rachel laid out the blanket so we could enjoy the last of the late afternoon sun. Getting clean again gave us both a renewed sense of confidence, and it wasn't long before our lips met, and we made wild, passionate love.

We rinsed off again, and Rachel suggested it would be fun to take a walk in the nude. Nobody could see us, and it was still light.

"Let's go somewhere we haven't been yet, and see what we find," she said, insinuating another romp would not be out of the question. "What do you say we try this direction?"

I was definitely game, and we strolled down a new path that took us across a pasture I hadn't seen before. We stopped every few yards for a kiss, reminders of how perfectly things turned out.

Squawk, squawk. Our last interlude was interrupted by a pair of vultures circling overhead. The birds flew low and dropped behind some high bushes around a bend. We wanted to see what they were fussing about and continued down the path.

"They are probably feasting on a dead r-r-raccoon or something else delicious," I joked. "I hope the sight of it won't freak you out."

"Oh, come on," she giggled. "Don't judge me by my reaction to those leeches. That was a whole different level of creepy."

The path turned to the left and we found ourselves at the fenced edge of the property. It was just the right place to grab another kiss, but when I tried, Rachel screamed and pushed me away.

"What d-d-did I do?"

She dropped to her knees and threw up on my bare feet. Confused, I turned back around to see what had upset her and was so revolted by what I saw, I threw up as well. A blackened corpse hung against the fence, melted skin peeling in places. In some spots, the skin was liquefied and oozed down the chain link like frosting.

I needed to know who it was, and I managed to pull myself together sufficiently enough to venture closer. The flesh was so warped I couldn't immediately tell; though, it was clear by the burnt skin that the person had been electrocuted. Then I saw the PF Flyers.

"My god, it's Tornado! She must not have realized the fence was on."

Rachel was still sobbing when I went back to console her, but under the circumstances I didn't know how successful I'd be. Even when I closed my eyes, I couldn't get the image of Tornado's charred fingers curled in that panicked grip out of my brain.

"Do you think she was really electrocuted?"

I gulped. "I don't see any other explanation. I'd guess she was trying to c-c-climb over the fence, though I can't imagine why. We all knew it was electrified, and at least that explains what caused the power outage."

"No electric fence could do that. My uncle raised cattle, and his ranch had one. We messed around with it when we were kids. Sure, you could feel a little shock, but electric fences don't electrocute people."

I remembered Ma mentioning Pa had to order special parts, and something about it being illegal. At the time, I thought she was joking, but it was no longer funny. What the hell was wrong with her that she thought it was acceptable to have a fence like this? I made up my mind that as soon as we got back to the house, I would call the police. Then I was going to leave and abandon my earlier plan to stick around. It was too dangerous to stay.

Rachel was shaking as she stared at Tornado's remains. "Are we just going to leave her up there like that?"

"What else can we do? The cops will want to see her the w-w-way she died."

"Don't you think it'll be obvious what happened? I'd feel better if we at least put her down on the ground. I won't be able to get the sight of her up there out of my mind if we don't."

She had a point. It would be clear to anyone seeing Tornado up there that she was electrocuted, and it did feel inhumane to leave her stuck in such a grotesque and humiliating pose. But getting her off the fence was difficult, and I was sorry the moment I started.

Her body did not come off the fence in one piece. Clothing kept her torso and legs together, but I had to peel the rest of her off in strips, much as I peeled the leeches off Rachel earlier.

The corpse oozed and dripped, beginning from my face down my chest and along my legs. In a twisted way, it was a blessing I was naked. Had I been wearing clothes, I would have had to burn them, and now I could wash off at the pump on the way back.

I respectfully lay Tornado down on the ground next to the fence and hoped we hadn't made a mistake. I'd seen enough detective shows to know that you weren't supposed to mess with evidence. I considered that, in a backwards sort of way, the cops might classify the death as a murder or at least manslaughter. Maybe they'd even arrest Ma for having an illegal fence.

When I washed at the pump again, I took my time and scrubbed more thoroughly. There was a solemnity to my ritual, a stark contrast to the giddy anticipation I felt when I washed earlier.

"At least this time, nobody stole our clothes," grumbled Rachel, grateful to be getting dressed.

We were both in shock, but by the time we reached the house I had whipped myself into a fury. I was going to call the cops myself. Ma was a little backwards, but I didn't believe for a moment that she was a fool, and I didn't trust her.

I barged right in. "I need to use your phone. Right now. Tornado's d-d-dead, and I'm calling the police."

"Goodness gracious, you both look a fright."

Rachel did most of the talking, and while she described our ordeal, I stared at the huge throw switch on the kitchen wall. Before all this happened, Rachel and I joked that it resembled a prop from a Frankenstein movie. Now, it turned my stomach. And it was in the *up* position, which I remembered meant *on*.

"You poor babies. It just breaks my heart to imagine how horrifying that must have been for you. But, don't you worry. I'll handle it, I promise you that."

"Do I smell coffee?" Peter called from the back hall, sounding jolly. "I'd kill for a cup."

I did a double take, astounded to see him emerging from what appeared to be a guest bedroom.

"Oh, sometimes Peter stays over," Ma said. "You know, when we have a lot of stuff to sort through. Coffee, everyone? I've just made a fresh pot. Good thing the stove cooks with gas and we don't need electricity."

Peter took a seat at the table next to her. "Did I interrupt something? You all seem so serious."

Ma took charge. "We lost a hiker to the fence today, Peter, or so they said."

I noted how calm she was as she poured the coffee. Despite hearing such tragic news, she didn't splash a drop.

Peter looked horrified. "You're sure she's dead?"

I thought again of the lifeless body we peeled from the fence. "Oh, we're sure."

"But electrocuted? That seems so unlikely."

"You're right, Peter. I don't usually turn the fence on. Only when I need to protect my hiker family. Like the other night, from them coyotes."

"Did you turn the power back off the next morning?"

"No, she didn't," I said, looking up at the throw switch. "You said yourself when it's up, it means the fence is on!"

"I d-d-doubt I told you that," Ma mimicked. "Land sakes listen to me. You've got me so flustered, I'm talking like you."

I thought she was making fun of me until she clutched her pearl necklace. "Honestly, on, off, up, down, I don't recall what either position means, anymore." She rattled on. "And my goodness, we've got warning signs up all over the place. Pa made sure of it."

Peter offered a bit of support. "You do tell the hikers not to go near the fence, don't you?"

"I'm a broken record," she replied, pouring herself another cup.

"You never told us once," I said, and Rachel nodded in corroboration.

"This is terrible, and I feel awful." Ma stood up. "I'll call Sheriff Toler. He'll know what to do." She pulled a hanky out of her bosom and dabbed at her tears. "I hate for anyone to see me like this," she choked.

"Yes, yes," Peter said, putting his hand on hers. "He'll straighten everything out."

Her face grew serious and she turned to me. "Where's the body?"

I went into detail of the messy business of getting her off the fence and the ground.

"So, you moved the body? Oh, dear. Sheriff Toler won't like hearing that."

"Well, we couldn't just leave her there, s-s-stuck to the fence."

"With your fingerprints all over her, you two will be implicated for sure. And knowing Toler, he'll want to hold you overnight, maybe even for months, until everything gets sorted out. You know how these things work."

At the thought of standing trial for murder, Rachel burst into tears. I didn't blame her. Tornado was more than a fellow hiker, she was a friend. Being accused of her murder was too much to contemplate.

"Say, I've got an idea. You poor kids shouldn't have to get caught up in all this. I think I can handle Toler by myself.

Been friends since we was yea high. He'll understand it was an accident." She looked at Peter. "Be a dear and run them into Harpers Ferry, will you? They can stay in Aunt Sally's old house till things blow over. Ain't nobody using it now. You can take my car."

I said we could be ready in twenty minutes or so, but Ma wanted us out right away. I asked if we could get paid before we left, and she said she'd send the money later with Peter.

"But we're both b-b-broke," I protested. "Please. How long could it take?"

Ma showed her exasperation with a long sigh as she lifted herself out of the chair. It seemed she leaned more heavily on her cane and took longer to cross the kitchen.

"Now where did I put that damned key?" she asked, as she removed a locked strongbox from a cabinet. "I swear I'm losing my mind. You didn't see it lying around, did you, Peter?"

"Ma, I'm surprised at you. Your father would not be happy to hear that foul language. He'd have washed your mouth out with soap."

Ma waved his criticism aside. "Well, who do you think taught me to use 'em?"

She felt around on the countertop in the vicinity of the strongbox, and then poked around in a drawer. She sighed and inched her way across the floor where she rummaged around in an old oak desk. Peter drummed his fingers as she picked through a jar of nuts and bolts.

He rolled his eyes. "Tell you what. This could take all day," he whispered to us with a wink. "I'll look for the key myself when I get back. Let's get you out of here right now."

He disappeared down the hall and returned moments later with the car keys, and then he hustled us out of the kitchen.

Rachel and I huddled together in the backseat of the ancient sedan, and she commented that she had never seen cloth upholstery. It was hot inside and feeling nauseous, and she rolled down the window for some fresh air.

As Peter coaxed the engine into gear, I threaded my arm through hers, and she rested her head against my shoulder. She closed her eyes, and I dropped a kiss on the top of her head.

The car rolled forward, and silently I thanked God I was once and for all on my way out of that god-forsaken farm.

15

My eyes stared vacantly out the window until I realized we weren't going down the driveway. "Where are we g-g-going?"

"Well, with the power down and everything, the front gate can't be opened, so I'm taking you out the back way."

I was pleased to hear of another way out and relieved that we were in good hands. Rachel's head bobbed up and down on my chest as the car crawled away from the house down the rough driveway. In the rearview mirror, I saw Peter smiling back.

"You kids are cute," he said. "I remember when Pa and I were your age. I couldn't wait to find a young lady. Never did, though."

I wasn't sure why he was bringing this up. I guessed he could tell how rattled we were, and he was trying to distract us. In any case, I welcomed the conversation.

"So, you knew Ma and Pa when you were younger?"

Peter laughed. "Yes, but I knew Pa better, and we referred to him as Cletus back then. We were rowdy teenagers and best friends."

I smiled as I imagined Peter as a rowdy teenager.

Peter laughed. "You know, I could tell you a funny story about that cabin Ma uses for her Lost and Found if you're interested."

Not waiting for a response, Peter leaped into his story with an energy that was admirable and clearly designed to take our minds off our troubles. It was back when they were boys, he said, maybe fifteen or sixteen.

"He brought me to that cabin," Peter told us, smiling as he reminisced. "Of course, in those days it wasn't falling down."

Inside there was a bed and not much else, but to two teenage boys, that was pretty neat. Under the mattress, though, was something even better. It was the first girlie magazine Peter ever saw, and it had been folded and re-folded and creased, an obvious sign that Pa's dad spent a lot of time with it. They were mesmerized by page after page of naked women in what were meant to be sexy poses. Some pictures showed them fornicating with men.

"A magazine like that one was so scandalous," said Peter. "Our impressionable young minds were forever tainted."

He and Pa were giggling at a picture of one woman with particularly enormous breasts when a large hand reached down in between them and yanked the magazine away. It was Grampa Winter, and he wasn't happy.

"I don't think I ever saw Cletus so pale. He thought we were both going to get a licking, and, if you pissed off a man like Grampa, you wouldn't be able to sit for days."

The two boys waited in horror as Grampa Winter thumbed through the pages. The boys thought he was getting angrier and angrier. Then the old man started laughing, and they were relieved.

Peter was through. "The end. Pretty good story, huh?"

"That's it? That's the whole story?"

"Oh, for heaven's sake. The cabin is why I started the story to begin with, wasn't it? Well, just when we thought we were home free, Grampa Winter opened a trapdoor in the floor, yanked us by the wrists and threw us down into a pit. He kept us locked down there overnight."

I sat up straight, jostling Rachel awake. "Wait, a trapdoor in the cabin f-f-floor? Why didn't we see it?"

"There used to be a rug covering the hatch. Probably still there."

Grampa Winter came back a few days later and opened it to let the boys out. He was all smiles and asked if they had a good time.

"How did you manage being down there in the p-p-pit for so long?"

"Oh, it was easy. There were candles and mattresses. We found where he kept his moonshine and more magazines like the one he took from us. The pit was always stocked with canned food, long enough to live down there for two weeks or so, not that anyone could hear you. The place was soundproof, though we never understood why."

"Is it still there?"

"I suppose so. Why wouldn't it be?"

My heart was pumping double time. Maybe it was crazy, but my gut told me that Daisy was there. I was never fully convinced that she'd left me, and, with this new information, it was possible she hadn't. While I couldn't imagine why she'd be hiding from us there, it was the only place I hadn't searched, and I knew I couldn't rest until I found out.

I shot forward in my seat, sending Rachel backward in an awkward tumble. Her head thumped against the window and she muffled a mild complaint.

"Will you t-t-take us there?"

"Sure. We can make a stop on the way."

"What are you talking about?" she objected. "We have to get out of here before the police come."

I was impatient. "Didn't you hear? We might be in luck. Peter told us about a room below the floor of the cabin, and I believe Daisy might be hiding there. They say the room is even soundproof. She could have been down there screaming her head off the whole time we were there!"

Rachel was angry. "I thought we were through with this Daisy craziness. Fine, we'll go check out this trapdoor. But after that, we *are* leaving. I can't stay here any longer."

I'd been so wrapped up in Peter's story and the new hope of finding Daisy, I'd forgotten about Tornado's corpse and that the reason we were in the car was to get away. I agreed to her terms.

Peter veered to the right and cut across a field to a well-worn grassy road. Unlike the treacherous path we took earlier, this one was clearly marked and free of barbed wire. Peter cruised through it with no trouble at all until eventually he turned onto a little gravel path that led right to the cabin.

"So, there was a road we could have taken all along?" Rachel asked.

"Ma didn't tell you? Odd. Well, here we are." The car rumbled and squeaked when he threw it into park.

I was the first to hop out. "Can you show me where the trapdoor is?"

"Easier to tell you," he said. "You'll find it across from the bed in the center of the floor. You two go on ahead. I'll wait here."

The inside of the cabin was as dark as before, but we agreed that something about the atmosphere was different. The disgusting stench was stronger than I'd remembered, and the place seemed dank and foreboding. Rachel clung to me with one arm and covered her nose with her other hand as we inched across the floor.

We tripped over something bunched up in the center of the room, and I guessed it was the rug Peter had mentioned, and I took it to mean somebody had pulled it away. At least that would make the trapdoor easier to find, especially in the dark.

My shoe felt the floorboard edge, and I stopped our forward motion. Despite the column of putrid air that rose from the floor, in the dark I could tell we were standing at the edge of the famous pit.

"Daisy? Daisy? Are you d-d-down there?" I called into the quiet abyss.

"Shh! Wait a minute. Do you hear something?"

We froze. I whispered back, "A noise from down there? Was it Daisy?"

"Shh. No, it wasn't her."

"Peter?"

"No, not him. Someone else coming from back there." She pointed into the darkness behind us. "I guess it was nothing."

I was eager to check out the pit. I hadn't heard anything and found it difficult not to say something.

"How do you think we get down there?" I asked. I leaned over and squinted. "Did you bring your flashlight?"

"No, we left everything in the car. I'll go get—"

She didn't have the chance to finish. Somebody behind us shoved her into me, and she toppled down into the pit, taking me with her. The floor was rocky and hard, and so was her landing.

Her body twisted, and her head jerked back, slamming her into a stone wall and knocking her out. I landed squarely on top of her, before bouncing off and rolling over to one side. My head hit the floor.

Bam! The heavy trapdoor slammed shut.

16

When I came to, I was in total darkness. The putrid stench in the pit made me nauseous, and the first thing out of my mouth was vomit. Bumping my head during the fall left me disoriented, and when I felt my hand resting on someone else's, for a moment I thought I was back in my tent.

"Daisy? Is that you? Oh, poor baby, you're c-c-cold."

I rubbed my hands on hers to warm her up and kissed the length of her bare arm, making exaggerated smooching sounds. When I didn't get a response to the kisses, I felt a twinge of irritation.

"Come on, Daisy, don't be that way. I don't blame you for being mad that I didn't come home that night, but I've got a big surprise for you."

I pulled the silver ring out of my pocket and felt for her ring finger. When it didn't slip on easily, I forced it on her pinkie and proclaimed we were engaged. I kissed her again and stroked her horribly matted hair until my fingers got snagged. When I pulled them away, her head snapped and dangled from its neck, leaking bodily fluids on my shirt.

"J-J-Jesus! What's this?" I wanted to throw up again, but my stomach was empty, and all I managed was dry heaves.

Rachel must have heard me retching as she regained consciousness at the other side of the pit. "What's going on? Where are we?" She sounded weak.

Her voice snapped me back to reality, and the particulars of our fall crashed back in vivid detail. In my delirium, I'd forgotten about Rachel, and now I wasn't even sure how to answer her question. I didn't understand what was going on, but one thing was clear. There was a dead body sitting next to me, and I didn't want to tell her, because I was afraid hearing about another corpse might send her over the edge.

"We're in the pit. Don't you remember f-f-falling?"

Rachel was angry. "Getting pushed is what I remember. What smells so nasty? I can hardly breathe."

I lied and claimed not to know.

"Ouch! Damn," she yelped, when she shifted her position. "I must have turned my ankle when I fell. Hurts like hell."

I reached out and found her leg and was relieved to feel denim. "You're still wearing jeans, aren't you?"

"Yes, of course, why?"

At least it wasn't another dead body. "Not sure why I asked," I lied again. I found her bare ankle and planted a kiss. "Feel better now?"

Rachel said her head pounded, and a hip ached from a big bruise she got in the fall. I kissed her ankle again and asked if the kisses were making it feel better.

"What are you talking about? What kisses?"

I dropped the foot I was kissing, and it landed on the floor with a thud. "Then who the hell's f-f-foot is this?"

I threw myself away from the leg and slammed against the wall. There were two bodies? No wonder it stank. I struggled to hide my panic, so I wouldn't alarm her, but the presence of the two decaying corpses made me gag.

"What's going on?" she snapped.

"Oh, yeah, sorry, for that," I responded. "The stench got to me, that's all."

"I don't mean the smell. I mean, if you're over there, who is lying here next to me?"

So much for keeping it to myself. "Rachel, I'm afraid we're not the only ones down here."

She shook the body, commanding it to wake up. When I told her the person was dead, she became hysterical and screamed, pounding her fists on the dead body's chest. Her shrieks became convulsions, and she threw up.

I knew it was going to be awkward, but I had to ask. "Is it Daisy? Could you tell?"

Rachel was furious. "How would I know? Is that all you think about? What about me? There may be a dead body next to me, but I'm alive!"

Her violent response was valid. She'd been through enough without the added stress of my insensitivity. I apologized, and, between sobs, somehow Rachel was able to collect herself.

"I have no idea if it's Daisy or not," she said. "But now I know this disgusting stench is coming from a dead body."

"From two, actually. There's another one lying next to me."

She shuddered again and kicked her feet on the floor, forgetting her twisted ankle. The pain was intense. "My god, what a nightmare. Why is this happening to us?"

We didn't speak for a few minutes. "Maybe the one next to you is Daisy," she said.

I hoped it wasn't, especially since I'd knocked its head off earlier. I groped around and found the body, and then came the tough part—I'd have to identify it by touch. I lowered my hand to the corpse, and it landed on the person's crotch.

"Hey, I found a book of matches," Rachel interrupted. "Maybe we can see what's going on." When she struck the first one, there was a momentary flare before it fizzled out. Same with the next one. "Hold on, I found another book."

"Never mind," I said. I didn't need any light to tell me the person was a dude.

"I found something better," she said.

The lit stub of a candle cast a steadier and more permanent light, but it flickered eerie shadows across the pit around us. It also illuminated the two corpses on the floor, neither of which was Daisy.

The one next to me was fat and round, its greenish skin somewhat decomposed. The other was fresher, but much, much more gruesome. Its head had been sliced off, and strings of wet veins seeped out of the bloody stump. I didn't see the head, but candlelight illuminated the bare-chested man's heavily tattooed arms.

"Oh, my God! This has to be the Australian's f-f-friend. He supposedly left days ago. What the hell is going on?"

Rachel's screams soon became whimpers as she curled into a ball on the floor. "I'm sorry Daisy's not down here," came her frail voice. "But maybe that means she's safe."

I pushed the dead man away to make a space, and she crawled over to me. She was so vulnerable, and I felt shameful for the way I'd treated her. I'd been as much a jerk to her as I'd been to CutePuppy124.

Suddenly, it dawned on me that my feelings for Rachel were real, and I pulled her close. I'd dragged her along, so I could look for another woman, and she had every right to blame me for being trapped in this hellhole.

"I'm the one who's sorry," I said. "I kept thinking Daisy would turn up and tell me all this was one big joke."

Rachel started to cry again.

I brushed my lips across her tear-stained cheeks. I found her lips, and when I kissed her, I felt her mouth smile back. "I promise I'll make his all up to you when we g-g-get out of here."

"No!" She spat and used her sleeve to wipe her mouth. "Your lips were all over that dead man's foot!"

Thanks to the candlelight, I now could see the outline of the trapdoor in the ceiling, and I was determined to find a way to open it. I was tall enough to touch the hatch with my fingertips but not tall enough to push it up, so Rachel climbed onto my shoulders and shoved against it as hard as she could.

It was too heavy and wouldn't budge. She tried folding her hands together to create a makeshift step, but she was too unsteady and couldn't hold my weight long enough for me to push against the door. The mattresses Peter spoke about had long-ago disappeared, and now there wasn't a stick of furniture or even a crate we could use as a step.

Rachel suggested something morbid. "You might not like this idea, but what if we use the bodies for a stool? We can stack one on top of the other."

I was struck at how naturally the macabre plan came out of her mouth as if it were the most ordinary solution in the world. This was a different side of the warm and empathetic Rachel I thought I knew.

Her suggestion was morbid, but I agreed to it. Standing on a dead man was nothing compared to handling Tornado's body. The Australian's friend lay directly under the trap door, so we hoisted the fatter one on top of him. Luckily, his plus size was exactly what I needed for more height. Once I got my balance, I could push the door open an inch, enough to shout through a call for help.

Without warning, the larger man's rib cage collapsed, and my feet sank into his stomach. "Shit, shit!" I lost my balance, and there was a sucking sound as I pulled my feet loose from the slimy entrails.

Furious, I slumped back down on the floor. "Where the hell is P-P-Peter? He should have come to check on us."

"I was thinking the same thing. Do you think he was the one who pushed us?"

"No, why would he do that?" I said. "He's been trying to help."

"Well, somebody did."

When the candle ran out of wax, I was out of ideas, and we were once again in total darkness.

"Hey, do you think this pit is actually soundproof? Seems a rather elaborate add-on for someone like Grampa Winter to install."

"We won't know if we d-d-don't try." We cupped our hands and hollered at the ceiling. We shouted and sang, and we kept it up until we ran out of steam and collapsed on the filthy floor.

The trap door cracked open, and we were thrilled by the sound of Peter's voice. "Are you two all right? I've been waiting in the car and wondered what could be keeping you."

"Jesus, where have you been? Never mind. Just g-g-get us out of here, will you? We've been trapped down here with a bunch of dead bodies."

"Dead bodies? Oh, my goodness. Why don't you use the ladder? That's what Pa and I used."

"What ladder? There's no ladder down here. Can't you just pull the door open the rest of the way?"

"It's heavy, but I'll try." He didn't sound confident.

He grunted and shuffled around as he re-positioned his feet for better leverage. "I'm sorry," he said. "I'm not strong enough anymore. I'll enlist someone to help. Maybe one of those big guys can pull it loose. Stay right where you are."

Bam! The trapdoor slammed shut, and Peter was gone.

"What the hell? Couldn't he have left the door open a b-b-bit?" I was livid, but our spirits were lifted knowing help was on the way. I snickered. "Can you believe he told us to stay put? Where could we go?"

We tried not to think about the corpses sharing the space with us, but the rotting stench was worse now that their guts had spilled out on the floor, so I pulled off my t-shirt and ripped it in strips and made us each a mask to cover our noses. We hugged in a comfortable silence for a few minutes, and then she spoke.

"Talk about alone time. It doesn't get much more private than this. Listen, I've been meaning to tell you something, and I wasn't sure how or when to bring it up. I think maybe now is the right time. I hope you don't take it the wrong way."

"Believe me. Nothing you say could faze me right now."

"Here goes." Her swallow was loud enough for me to hear. "We met before, you know, before the farm."

"Huh? We did?"

"Not met, exactly. But we were sort of a couple."

I had no idea where she was going with her story, and I floated a joke. "I think I would remember. Just how hard did you hit your h-h-head when you fell?"

"I'm serious. And by the way, you're even cuter in person. Not now, of course. Right now, you're a mess."

"Yeah, well you've looked better, too. Wait, I'm confused. You said we were a couple, and you're acting like we just met."

"Come on. Don't you understand? We only stopped talking a month or so ago."

I didn't follow.

"It's me, silly! CutePuppy124."

I scooted as far away from her as I could before slamming against another wall. I could hardly connect the dots of what she was telling me. It was too wild. "Holy shit! Are you insane? Why didn't you tell me before?"

She started to cry again. "Aren't you happy? I thought you would understand."

128

"Understand what? You lied to me, and I trusted you. God, I think I was in l-l-love with you."

"How do you think I felt?" she snapped. "I loved you, too. I know a bunch of stuff came up, but I really did try to meet in person. It's just that things came up that made it impossible. When I had car trouble that day, I was sure you'd come to help me. Instead, you disappeared. You broke my heart, Strider."

I flashed back to the first time I remembered speaking to her at the farm. *Don't you remember me?* At the time, I thought it was an odd thing to say. How could I have known what CutePuppy124 looked like? And why would I expect to see her at the farm? Being here was so out of context.

"You broke my heart again when someone said you were going to marry someone else, so soon. Do you have any idea how embarrassing that was for me, and how crushed I was to find out how little I meant to you? How could I tell you the truth after finding that out?"

I wasn't angry. Rachel stood by me faithfully, even when I asked her to help me find the woman I'd used to cheat on her. I'd made up my mind to rekindle the relationship anyway. Now it would be easier.

"I'm sorry," I said. "I love you. I has to be f-f-fate that we both ended up here. Can we start over?"

I turned and slid across the floor to the stack of bodies. It took me some fumbling in the dark to find the right hand. "I've got something for you," I said, producing the silver ring. I didn't tell her that when I pulled the ring off the dead man's pinkie, the guy's finger came off with it. I tried to slip it on Rachel's finger.

"Don't you even think about putting it on me. That ring is bad luck!"

I was disappointed. "Yeah, we wouldn't w-w-want any of that."

"Don't you think we should talk about how these hikers got here?" she asked. "They didn't just come here to die on their own."

"I don't know. They could have fallen in by mistake, like we did."

"And then one of them cut off his own head? Come on, don't be stupid. We didn't fall. Someone around here is deliberately killing hikers. They're killing them and stealing their stuff."

"Then who are these two? If you're right, Tornado and D-D-Daisy should be here, too."

"I know this doesn't explain everything, but Ma has to be behind all this. I bet she arranged for us to die down here, too."

Footsteps on the floor above threw us into a panic, thinking she had come to kill us. Rachel grabbed the ring from my hand and slipped it on her finger. "Screw her. Let her try, and if she wants to take us on, we'll fight her as a couple."

I underestimated her. All traces of fear had left her voice, and her ferocity was striking. Ma was going to meet her match. I was glad Rachel and I were on the same side.

17

When the trapdoor opened, someone was shining a flashlight down on my face, but I couldn't see past the blinding light to tell who it was. At first, I thought Ma was coming to do us in for good, but the coughing and gagging I heard was deep and masculine.

"Is anybody down there? God, what's that horrible smell?"

I was ecstatic, and when my eyes adjusted to the light, I saw Red leaning into the space with his arm outstretched, ready to help us out. I held Rachel steady on her good foot and he easily hoisted her up.

He was about to lay her on the cot, but she insisted on being taken outside so she could breathe real air again. He left her on the porch and took a deep breath before coming back for me. In no time, all three of us were safely outside the cabin.

"I hate to ask, but is there anything else from down there you need?"

"What I need," Rachel said, "is to forget everything that happened in that god-forsaken place."

By her swollen ankle, I could tell she wouldn't be able to walk, and I was grateful when Red scooped her up and carried her down the gravel road to the car path across the field, past the cemetery to the campsite, where he lowered her on the grass near the campfire. We sat quietly on the stumps and stared into the fire.

"I didn't think you were ever coming," I said. "P-P-Peter left us hours ago."

"Peter? Who's Peter?"

"Ma's friend. He wasn't strong enough to lift open the trapdoor, and he left us down there to get help. Said it would take a big g-g-guy, and we assumed he meant you. We were waiting down there all day."

"I still don't know who you're talking about, but I'm shocked the old lady has friends. But to answer your question, nobody told me."

"So, how did you find us?" Rachel asked.

He said the last time he saw us, we were headed off somewhere with towels, and when we didn't come back, he began to worry.

"It wasn't like I was stalking you or anything, but with so many hikers disappearing left and right, I got suspicious. Tornado, for example. I haven't seen her all day."

Rachel and I shared a loaded look, but we let him continue before we gave him the bad news. He said Ma's old beat-up jalopy caught his eye, too, as it rumbled slowly across a field, because he remembered seeing it in the barn and couldn't believe it even ran. He couldn't identify the driver, but he recognized Rachel and me in the backseat.

"I guess the driver must have been this Peter you're talking about."

The direction the car took intrigued him, too, because he hadn't realized there was a road through that part of the farm. When he saw we weren't in the back seat when the car returned, he figured we'd gotten a ride to Harpers Ferry.

"I remember thinking that it would have been nice for you to say goodbye, but frankly I expect you to." He looked at Rachel. "We had our differences."

Since our tents were still up and given the fuss I made when my stuff was stolen earlier, I could understand how he was curious we'd left anything behind, at least, on purpose. He wondered where the car had taken us, because it wasn't gone long enough to make a round trip to town. And he thought it was weird it came back the same way, and not through the front gate.

"None of this made any sense. I was about to take a break, so I decided to see where the car went. The old Plymouth was heavy and left deep tracks that were easy to follow, and they led me to the cabin. I didn't hear anything inside, and I was about to leave, when I tripped on the trapdoor latch. I opened it, and that's when I saw you guys.

It was a damn good thing, too, or we'd still be trapped. "You saved our lives, Red. How can we thank you?"

"You can start by telling me how you ended up down there."

Rachel took him through the horrifying sequence of events, beginning with our discovery of Tornado's body. When she was through, Red stood.

"I've heard enough. We're getting out of here right now. Ma's car is back in the barn, and if the keys aren't in it, it'll be a piece of cake to hotwire the old clunker."

There was no time to spare, and we gave ourselves five minutes to collect the rest of our things and meet in the barn. Most of our stuff was already in the trunk, or had been, when Peter took us to the cabin.

"Now what? How do you p-p-propose we open the gate? And if the power to the fence is on, then what?"

"If nothing else, the car gives us options, so let's worry about that when we get there," Red said, taking charge.

I volunteered to drive, and the others piled in. Red had started the car, but I couldn't figure out how to shift it into gear.

"Can you drive stick?"

"Shit, no."

"Then move over. I'll drive."

He drove us out of the barn, and we headed straight to the nearest part of the fence, ignoring the driveway and the gate. He parked as close as to it as he could, and we found that standing on the roof only left a climb of about four feet. Red and I knew we could climb over on our own, and between the two of us we could lift Rachel over, too, if the power to the fence was off. But since we couldn't be certain, I agreed to be the guinea pig and test the current. A quick swipe of my finger wouldn't hurt, and it would tell me a lot. After what I'd been through, I was feeling invincible.

"Ouch!" It was much more than a tingle. Ma was right, the fence was packing a lot of juice, and now we'd have to change our plan.

It was my idea to bash right through it. The old car was built like a tank, and if we started back far enough and got up enough speed, we could charge at the fence like a battering ram. Worse case, it would short it out. Either way, we'd be home free.

"It sounds like a horrible idea, but I don't see we have any other choice," Red said. "We can't exactly ask the old lady to open the gate."

Rachel was uncomfortable with the plan, but I felt the decision to take such a drastic measure had to be unanimous. We didn't want to leave her behind, and I was glad when she finally agreed to go along.

I rode shotgun and Rachel climbed in the back. Red backed the car up around fifty yards and was about to put it in gear, when she stopped him. She leaned over the seat and gave us each a quick kiss on the neck. "Just in case."

Red had one more instruction. "Look, this jalopy doesn't have seatbelts, so Strider, hop in the backseat with Rachel. You'll be safer."

He pulled on the knob to turn on the headlights. He threw it in gear and slammed the accelerator to the floor. In the backseat, Rachel and I clasped hands and held our breath as we sped straight at the fence. When we were twenty feet away, Rachel squeezed her eyes shut.

The impact was explosive and colossal. Sparks flew, metal crunched, the windshield shattered, and car parts of all kinds sailed off into the air. The headlights went out before the hood popped open, revealing the hissing radiator.

Slumped over and pinned in by the steering wheel, Red never saw the orange licks of flame that shot out of the mangled front end and both sides. He couldn't hear Rachel screaming directly behind him, either. Her door was sprung, and it took a strong kick from her good foot to force open. She scrambled out of the car, and, ignoring her turned ankle, pulled me out of the wreckage by my armpits.

"I'm going back for Red!" she said, after I was safely on the grass.

Smoke billowed out in giant columns from the giant fireball that used to be Ma's car. Rachel managed to yank Red free of the steering wheel, and by the look of him, it wasn't clear if he was alive or dead.

The windshield was too old to be made of safety glass, and he glittered from a million fragments covering his body. He was lucky his thick beard deflected many of the pieces, but multiple long and lethal shards pierced his face above the beard, and he was bleeding profusely everywhere.

Loud buzzing from a transformer provided an ominous soundtrack to the sparks dancing between the metal of the fence and the fenders of Ma's car. By now, we were all on the grass a safe distance away but neither Rachel nor I paid attention to the fireworks display.

I carefully picked pieces of glass from Red's face, while she attempted to stop his bleeding elsewhere with bandages she'd made from her filthy shirt.

"Don't take that one out," she said, pointing to the large piece stuck in his shoulder. "It went in too deep. I'm afraid he might bleed out."

"Red, can you hear m-m-me?"

His eyes fluttered open and closed in what I took as a positive response. "Hang in there, buddy."

I couldn't help but think that if he died, it would be my fault. Ramming the fence was my idea.

Rachel was troubled. "We have to call for help. Even if we do get away from this farm, t-shirt scraps aren't going to get him all the way to a hospital."

I remembered the fence and wondered if we'd been successful. With the car up in flames and Red severely injured, I'd forgotten our mission was to crash through it. I left her to care for him and ran through all the smoke and steam to see if we had broken through, devastated to find it still standing proud and strong as a fortress.

"What do we do with him now? He's starting to shake."

"He saved our lives, and it's our turn to help him, and that can only mean taking him back to Ma." When I saw her horrified expression, I corrected myself. "To her house, I m-m-mean, to use her phone. It's obvious that she never called the police, or they would be here by now, so we'll do it ourselves."

"And that proves she's behind all this, all the murders, everything," Rachel said. "We were meant to be one of her statistics, and I'll bet we're still in her crosshairs."

In the meantime, I knew if we didn't apply antiseptic to Red's cuts, an ambulance might not do him any good. There was only so much shirt to go around, and some of his wounds were bleeding through. Rachel said she knew where Ma kept her first aid kit. We'd use what she had to slow the bleeding enough until help came.

I was nervous to move him, so as gently as I could I looped an arm around and brought him to his feet, relieved when he screamed in protest. At least we knew he was conscious.

My knees buckled almost immediately. Red was a big guy, but until I had to carry him, I had no idea how heavy. Rachel swooped in to grab his other arm, supporting half his body the best she could, ignoring her ankle that screamed in agony, and together we shambled down the driveway for the excruciating journey to the farmhouse.

18

Somehow, we got Red settled in a recliner on the front porch, where we felt we had the best chance to stabilize him. His eyes were closed, his breathing nearly imperceptible. To anyone else he might have appeared dead, but to us his weak pulse was promising.

Just then, Sparky rounded the corner of the house and asked what we were doing.

"We're in a hurry and I don't have time to break it down. I've got to go inside and call the police. It was a terrible accident. T-T-Take care of him, will you?"

During the long slog down the driveway, Rachel and I came up with another escape plan. While I distracted Ma, Rachel was going to sneak past her and use the phone. On its face, the idea was simple, but Ma was apparently capable of taking out all those hikers, even with a bum leg, so we had to execute it flawlessly. Since Sparky agreed to pitch in, not having to stay with Red would make our job that much easier.

We stopped in the toolshed to pick up anything we could use as weapons. Since nobody was working, it was jam-packed with shovels and hoes—whatever we wanted. Rachel grabbed a small garden trowel, which I thought looked ineffective.

"Easier to handle," she explained. "If Ma is standing right next to me, a huge shovel won't do much good."

I dropped the big spade I had been holding. Rachel's eye caught a curious object hanging on the back wall, and she remarked at how it resembled Ma's cane, but I was more interested in the machete dangling on a hook next to it and gave it a test swing. She was impressed with my choice.

"Twisted, like her. I like it."

We decided Rachel would only report that a hiker was seriously injured, and we needed an ambulance. She wasn't to mention anything about Tornado or any of the other bodies either, because we didn't want to risk Ma turning the story around to pin the murders on us. The plan was to leave as soon as the ambulance arrived.

Rachel graced me with a quick kiss. "Remember, if you want to sneak up on her, go at her right side. She's deaf in that ear."

I brandished my machete. "Ready? Let's go try to survive a fight with an old lady."

This time we didn't bother to knock and made no effort to be quiet. For all I knew, Ma was waiting patiently for us behind the door with an ax, so it was better to surprise her. What we found instead was Ma leaning against a counter with her back to the room. She was stirring a cup of hot tea and whistling a strange little tune as if the day was unremarkable.

"You were gone for an awful long time, Peter," she said, turning. "I was beginning to think you—"

She seemed genuinely astonished to see the two of us. I'd never witnessed her flinch before, even when I gave her the horrifying news of Tornado's gruesome death, so I was amazed when the teacup slipped out of her hand and shattered on the floor.

"Now see what you did!" she cried, waving at the mess. "Didn't your mamas ever teach you to knock? You two gave me a fright!"

Her nonchalance infuriated me. She was the obvious villain and still wasn't willing to acknowledge it. "I'll b-b-bet we did. Surprised to see us alive, huh?"

Ma kept her cool and calmly swept up the shattered bits of cup and saucer. "This belonged to my Aunt Sally," she lamented, fondling a piece of the china. "Part of a set, and irreplaceable."

Rachel's eyes zeroed in on the old, powder-blue-corded princess telephone on the counter. When Ma walked toward the storeroom to retrieve her dustpan, Rachel made her move and repositioned herself within arm's distance of the phone. It was my turn.

"We're taking you in, Ma. We know about the bodies in the pit—and god knows how many others you've got stashed around the place—and starting r-r-right now, this demented game you've been playing is over!"

She sniffed at Rachel's weapon. "You're going to take me down with a garden trowel?"

"Not with that, with this!" I pulled the machete from behind my back and pointed it at her. "Rachel, make the call!"

"Yes, by all means, Rachel, make your call." Ma's hand was still on the doorknob to the storeroom. "Unless you'd rather I show your boyfriend what's behind Door Number One?"

I didn't understand, but I kept my weapon aimed at her. "What is she talking about?"

Rachel's face turned white. "I don't know what she means," she said, holding up the receiver. "But, um, the phone is dead, so I can't use it, anyway."

"Good girl," Ma laughed as she opened the storeroom door.

I guessed she was about to get a weapon of her own, and I moved in, holding my machete like a fencer, ready to lunge. "Don't try anything," I threatened. "I won't hesitate to use this!"

She laughed at me again. "You two are in over your heads. When you see the surprise I've got, you may change your mind."

With one swift motion she reached in and yanked Daisy out from behind the door. She was nearly unrecognizable. There were huge bags under her eyes, and her dark waves of hair were limp and oily. Her clothes were filthy, and I could smell her from the other side of the kitchen. Her dilated pupils were still adjusting to the light, and it was difficult to tell where they were looking.

I didn't understand why Ma had her locked up, but I didn't care. I was overjoyed.

"Daisy! You're alive!"

"You bitch!" she screamed, trying to wiggle free of Ma's arm lock.

"You settle down!" Ma demanded. She produced a long knife and held it to Daisy's throat. "One more word out of you, and it's curtains."

Her wild eyes darted around the room and zeroed in on me. "Where have you been? I thought you'd at least try to find me! She kidnapped me!"

I moved closer. "Let her go, Ma, or I'll k-k-kill you!"

"You're too much of a c-c-coward," she mocked, baiting me. "I dare you."

I'd had all I could take and lunged at her with my machete, intending to drive it through her.

"Strider, don't be like her!" Rachel warned.

She threw herself across the room and slammed into Ma's shoulder, which spun her around, setting Daisy up as her human shield. Ma lost her chokehold and dropped the knife, and, in the chaos, propelled Daisy forward.

I couldn't pull back in time, and she fell into my outstretched blade, which pierced her neck and sank into her throat. When it tore through the other side, blood erupted from her severed arteries and splattered against the kitchen wall. She looked at me in bewilderment before sinking to the floor.

"*No!*" I bellowed, dropping down beside her. Her frozen eyes stared up at me as I cradled her blood-soaked head.

"Oh my God, oh my God. I just k-k-killed somebody."

Ma struggled to her feet and dusted herself off. Then she corrected me. "Somebodies. You killed two. Daisy, and her baby."

PART THREE

19

D ragging Red all the way to the garden from the house was out of the question. He was simply too big for Sparky to manage. A heavy load like that was a chore better suited to his trusty wheelbarrow, not brute strength. Besides, he'd been plenty busy all day and was tired.

The skies had been threatening a downpour for days, and gauging from the ominous clouds, he sensed the rain would come for real at any moment. That would complicate things, because he would need to finish the job before it started. Weather or no weather, he had no choice. He'd told Strider he would take care of Red, and he always kept his word.

With one shove, Red tumbled into the wheelbarrow, and straining under the massive weight, Sparky trudged off to the garden. At least he wouldn't have to dig a grave from scratch. That was the part he hated. Red had been digging overtime for a couple of days and there were plenty of vacant vegetable plots he could use. He chuckled at the idea of Red digging his own grave.

It'll be a rush job, no matter what. But at least this one's all together, not like that girl from the fence. So many pieces. Collecting them took forever.

His daydreaming came to an abrupt halt when his wheelbarrow hit a bump and he lost his grip on one of the handles. The wheelbarrow started to tilt to one side and, because of Red's weight, Sparky couldn't stop it from tipping over. Red spilled to the ground.

"Rats!" he said, when he thought of how hard it would be to lift the big man back in. He jokingly apologized and took full blame for not paying attention.

Suddenly, there was a loud crash inside the house followed by a couple of screams.

"Hold on! Did you say something?" He stared at Red's face for a second, believing he'd heard a grunt. "Ha-ha, of course you didn't. It must have been that racket going on up in the kitchen, and, let me tell you, it sounds like a real hoo-ha. I'll find out what happened soon enough."

When he finished righting the wheelbarrow, he sighed. "I was hoping to take a little nap, but apparently my day isn't over yet. At least you'll have peace and quiet. I have a feeling they're going to need me up there when I'm done with you."

He dumped Red on the grass and rolled him over into the nearest plot. It was shallow, and he fell to the bottom with a muted thump.

"I could have picked a deeper one, I suppose, and that's what I get for being in such a hurry. Hope you don't mind. I wanted to cover you up before you got rained on. I'll make it up to you by putting on plenty of topping to make it look nice."

When he finished burying Red, he tossed the shovel aside and dusted off his hands. It wasn't his finest work, but it would do the trick. The house was silent now, and he guessed everyone had settled down. Maybe he could take that nap, after all, and he closed his eyes.

"I wonder what Ma will plant here," he mused. "Maybe radishes. Yeah, that's it, Red's Radishes."

20

I cradled Daisy's head in my lap. "She was p-p-pregnant?" I watched her life ooze out over the linoleum floor.

Ma rolled her eyes. "Men are so clueless. It was obvious the day you two first walked down my driveway. A mother can always tell when a woman's carrying." She reached into the cabinet for another of Aunt Sally's teacups. "Besides, she told me."

"But how could she be? We were only together a couple of weeks."

Ma sniffed. "Who said it was yours? She blamed it on that ex of hers. Didn't sound like a very nice guy, if you ask me."

"An ex? How come you knew she had an ex, and I didn't?"

She smirked. "Hmm. That's odd. Dani wouldn't shut up about him. She was up here every day, you know, and we had lots of time for girl talk."

I was torn. While I hated that Daisy had been held prisoner, I felt better that she hadn't abandoned me. I was angry that she kept her pregnancy from me, but at least the mystery of the rushed engagement was solved.

As I stared down at her lifeless body, I wondered what else she'd lied about. And something else started to bug me. Was I the only one on the planet who didn't call her Dani?

"There's so much about her I d-d-don't understand."

"Nothing complicated about it at all. Girl was preggers and scared. Why do you suppose she wanted you to marry her so fast? At least that's what she told me." Ma sipped her tea. "Did you think it was because you're such a catch?"

"Now I wonder if she l-l-loved me at all."

"Who cares if she was pregnant?" Rachel's sudden outburst pierced the conversation. "You *killed* her!"

"What do you mean, *I* killed her? Y-Y-You pushed her into my machete!"

"I did not. I was trying to keep you from doing something you would regret. How was killing Ma going to help anything? Admit it. You're the one who slashed her neck."

Rachel had a point, and I knew my defense was weak. I killed Daisy in front of everyone. "Technically, I was only holding the machete, and you all saw that it was an accident. So, now what do we do?"

"What we came to do. We're going to call that ambulance. Red is still out on the porch half dead."

Ma laughed. "Oh, yes, a great idea. Why don't you kill two birds with one stone and tell 'em to bring the sheriff, while you're at it. And you thought you were in trouble before." She strode confidently to the stove to put the kettle on, proving she maintained the upper hand.

Daisy's head clunked to the floor when I stood. "She's right. We can't stick around. We're going to have to make a r-r-run for it, and Ma is going to help."

"I am? How?"

"By l-l letting us."

I took her by surprise when I jumped her from the back. She protested but didn't resist much as I hauled her across the floor into the storeroom. A straight-backed wooden chair sat in a smelly mess of feces and urine in the center of the room, and ropes that once bound Daisy gathered on the floor around its legs. I called for Rachel to help.

"How poetic!" I said, tossing Ma on the chair. "Let's see how you like being t-t-tied up in the same room as Daisy."

I held her down while Rachel expertly tied her hands and feet. She was remarkably good at it, and when I half-joked about her having done it before, she dismissed the praise and gave credit to the Girl Scouts for her expertise, adding that she always won trophies for being the best at tying knots. I asked Ma why she kidnapped Daisy, but she didn't answer and only laughed.

"What does it matter now?" Rachel asked, rushing me out of the room when we were finished. "She's capable of anything. Let's just go."

"Look who's talking," Ma shouted from the other room. "I'm not the one who left a corpse on the kitchen floor."

The kitchen was a mess. Daisy's blood had drained into a large pool in the middle of the floor, but I wasn't concerned. Cleaning up the body and the blood was now Ma's problem. I planned to leave an anonymous note at the first police station I found, and if the authorities got there before she had a chance to clean it up and dispose of Daisy's body, she'd have a lot of explaining to do.

"Oh, my god! I forgot about Red." Rachel hobbled a little too fast on her way to the door and slipped on the blood, landing with a splash. Her entire backside up to her neck was slick with brownish goop. She tried to stand up but slipped and fell again, this time getting blood on her front.

Hearing the fall, Ma called out again. "Hope you're not planning to take off and leave your dead girlfriend lying there stinking to high heaven."

"I'm afraid she's your problem now. And what's one more dead body and a little more b-b-blood to you? We're outta here. Nice knowing you."

"You two are even dumber than I thought. Eventually, someone is going to stop by and see me tied up, and I'm not the one they'll care about. Both of you left fingerprints all over the place. If you think you're going to get away with murder, you gotta bury the bodies you kill and clean up the evidence."

It was a nightmare for me that wouldn't end but, once again, I knew she was right. We would have to conduct a thorough cleaning of the place before we left.

Rachel suggested we bury Daisy in the garden plot Ma was going to use for Daisy's Dill. She acknowledged it was a bit macabre, but since there was already a hole we could use, all we'd need to do was cover her over with dirt, so the job wouldn't take long. Besides, we couldn't leave her on the floor, and I hadn't come up with a better idea.

"The sign Daisy painted for herself can even be her headstone," she said with a bit of levity.

Although I didn't find it funny, I gave her plan my stamp of approval. Using a vegetable plot would save time, and I knew Rachel was in a hurry to get medical treatment for her foot. In recent hours, she complained it had become more excruciating than ever.

She grabbed Ma's first aid kit and limped for the porch. "I'll see what I can do to tide Red over until the professionals arrive. I hate to leave him behind, but hopefully help will come before too long."

"No. Leaving Red is out of the question," I said. "Now that Ma is tied up, I've got time to figure out a way to bring him with us."

With Rachel out of the room, I was glad for a moment of privacy, but as I gazed at Daisy's crumpled and lifeless body, I worried about my emotional detachment. I'd been ready to marry this woman, and now her death seemed like nothing more than a mild inconvenience. In the last hour, I'd been elated to learn she hadn't abandoned me after all but devastated that she'd been lying to me all along. I was relieved she wasn't another of Ma's victims but horrified that I ended up killing her myself. I supposed my detachment must have come from shock. It was simply too much to process, and I couldn't understand what was going on, let alone how I felt about it. Worst of all, the one person who could help me sort through this mess was dead on the floor in front of me.

I kissed her hand one final time. Even with blood splattered across her face she looked so innocent, and I was reminded of how young she was. And while I felt foolish when my eyes filled with tears, it was a relief to realize I could still care.

The thought of entrusting someone as smelly, crude, and clueless as Sparky to supervise her burial suddenly seemed unacceptable, and, with one last gesture of gallantry, I scooped her up in my arms and carried her to the garden, where I set her on the grass.

Sparky was lounging in the bed of his wheelbarrow when we arrived. "Is that Daisy you've got?" he asked. "Great that you found her. I forgot how pretty she was. I—"

"Sparky, stop talking. Daisy is dead."

He squinted. "Oh, I can see that now that you're closer. Say, she took great care of her skin."

"Listen, can you help me? We've got to bury her fast. As soon as we finish, Rachel, Red, and I are getting out of here. If you're smart, you'll come with us, too."

"Red? Um, I, he—"

"Sparky, we don't have time for a big discussion, okay? Will you help me or not?"

He agreed, and we dumped Daisy into the nearest hole. We were filling dirt around her body when Rachel limped over from the house. She sounded frantic.

"Red's not on the porch. What did you do with him, Sparky?

I was confused. "What does she mean? You were supposed to t-t-take care of him for me."

"Hey, settle down. I did," he replied. "He's over there. See his sign? You'll have to tell me how he died sometime. Didn't think it was possible, but he was more scratched up than me, ha-ha."

I panicked. "D-D-Died? When? And over where?"

"Well, it says Rachel's Radicchio now, but when I have time, I'll repaint it to read 'Red's Radicchio.' Nice that we already had something that started with 'R.'"

"Wait a minute! You buried him?"

"Well, yeah. You told me to."

"Good god, Sparky. I said to take care of him, not bury him. He was in c-c-critical condition but he was alive."

"I assumed you meant to get rid of his body. Anyway, he looked dead to me."

Rachel froze. "He was okay when we left him with you. Are you sure he was dead?"

Sparky gazed over at Red's grave and hesitated before he answered. "Pretty sure. He was a wreck, though. How did he get so much glass in his face?"

I recounted the details of plowing into the fence, struck by how Sparky followed the story without expressing any emotion.

"Oh, when I saw that mess, I wondered how Ma's car ended up there. Ramming through the fence was your idea? Gee, that was awful dumb. That fence is real strong. And you let him drive? Man, I'd feel terrible about that. It's like you killed him yourself."

"Sparky, I—"

He interrupted me this time. "So, what happened to your girlfriend here? Did you kill her, too?"

"Ma did," Rachel lied before I had to. "In the kitchen, a minute or two ago. Slashed her neck with a kitchen knife."

"That doesn't sound like Ma to me."

I was no longer listening. My eyes were glued to Daisy's dirty face and blood-soaked clothing when a clump of foul-smelling compost dropped on her face. I asked Sparky what the hell he was doing because Daisy's grave didn't call for compost.

"It does if we're going to plant dill in it," he said, continuing to layer until the grave was full. "Don't worry about planting the seeds. I'll do that later. Planting is the best part! I just love watching all those little sprouts pop out of the ground. And once Ma cans everything? Delicious!"

"Finishing touches," Rachel said, and she staked a post into the ground. It read *Daisy's Dill*. "I snagged it from the bed it was on."

The three of us stepped back to admire our handiwork. The grave was the perfect solution for hiding the evidence. It blended with every other filled bed in the garden. All that remained was to clean up the mess in the kitchen. Then, no one would suspect a thing.

I was afraid Rachel wouldn't be able to walk. She complained that the pain was so intense, it was making her dizzy, so before I left to clean the kitchen, I made her lie down on the grass, with her foot elevated. It was grotesquely swollen, and I guessed the injury was more than a sprain.

Her foot was battered, bruised, and bleeding after miles of walking on it, and the sock had disintegrated. I offered her one of my own, but it was too small, and, as gently as I tried to fit it over her foot, she screamed in agony.

"She can have one of mine," Sparky said, kicking off his boots. "I've got big feet. Everybody says so." He sat down on Daisy's grave to pull them off. Rachel recoiled at the thought of wearing one of his filthy socks, and she grimaced as he slipped it on.

"Thanks, Sparky. I'm sure if Rachel was feeling better, she'd tell you herself how m-m-much she appreciates it."

He announced matter-of-factly that he was taking the wheelbarrow back to the compost heap, and, after he left, I thought of how strange it was that the kid was so calm about burying two human beings. But I was also grateful. Thanks to him, there would be no evidence for the police to find. We considered asking him again if he was going to leave with us, because Rachel was concerned that something bad could happen to him.

Bringing Sparky along sounded practical. I hadn't figured out how we were going to escape yet, and without Red, I welcomed the extra hands. Since he was complicit in burying two dead bodies, I wasn't worried about him ratting us out.

What did worry me was the huge mess in the kitchen. Rachel would be of no help since she was too sore to leave her spot in the garden, so I'd have to clean it all up on my own. I dug around in all the places people commonly kept cleaning supplies but finding anything recognizable proved futile, and I had to ask Ma.

"Land sakes! I don't use anything off the shelf. Imagine the risk we'd run from all the dangerous chemicals they use. We Winters always make our own from scratch. With me tied up in here, you'll have to do the same."

From her chair in the storeroom, Ma bossed me as I rounded up her list of lye, vinegar, lemon and countless other ingredients. Her directions were sometimes vague, and I had to ask her to clarify so often that shouting around corners frustrated me. To save time, I dragged her chair into the doorway, so she could face the kitchen and monitor my work.

"No, no! Not all at once! Don't you know anything about chemistry? Start with the vinegar, and then add the baking soda, *slowly*, one teaspoon at a time. Any quicker and *kablam!* The whole place gets blown to Timbuktu."

Though I was quite sure she was exaggerating, I heeded her warning, just to be sure. Her badgering didn't stop. I'd mopped floors since I was a kid, but she criticized that, too, insisting that I'd have to get down on my hands and knees— all I was doing now was smearing it around, she said.

I ignored her and kept mopping my way, until I found I'd wasted the better part of an hour doing exactly what she said. I was pushing blood around the kitchen, rather than cleaning it up, and I realized she was right. From then on, I paid more attention to her suggestions, though her style was downright patronizing.

"Now there's a big circle of blood right there under the chair leg," she said, although she had to see I was already scrubbing it.

I gritted my teeth. "Yes, Ma, I know."

"And don't forget to rinse your sponge off or it'll just hold onto all that blood."

"Yes, I know that, too."

I never imagined it would take so long, and I wiped my forehead when I thought I was finished.

Ma gestured with her chin. "You missed the baseboards. Even with his cataracts, I guarantee it'll be the first thing Sheriff Toler will see."

Again, she was right. There was blood all over them. I went back to work, scrubbing until that blood was gone. Once I was done, she reminded me to scrub the corners. After that phase, she told me to wash down the counters and the cabinet doors, too. After a while, I could no longer tell if what she told me to clean was necessary, or simply her way of having me detail her entire kitchen.

It was humiliating to have my every move criticized by the enemy I was holding captive. When I finished, I was thrilled to stash her back into her prison cell.

"Okay, this is it. I'm locking you up and throwing away the key." I slammed the door behind me. In a few seconds, though, I was back in. Red-faced, I reminded her she still had the key and demanded she hand it over.

"I don't have it. Search me. Pat me down if you want," she taunted. "If you're tired of cradle-robbing, you might like a full-figured woman for a change."

I wasn't about to give her the satisfaction of pawing through her pockets, so I contented myself with slamming the door again.

Before I left, I had one more thing to do. Flip the monster switch and kill the power to the fence. It was in the up position, which I remembered meant it was on. I assumed the handle would be hard to move, and like Igor in the movies, I'd need to use both hands, but I was surprised how easily I flipped it off.

At last we were on our way.

21

"I wish Red was still here," Rachel said. She was just waking up when I returned to the garden.

I put an arm around her shoulder. "I know, I miss him, too."

"Oh, I didn't mean I missed him, like missing someone. I meant that he would be handy to have around. He could carry me."

I removed my arm, disgusted that she could be so cold, and frustrated we didn't have a plan to escape. The unexpected headlights of a car rumbling fast toward us were blinding. It skidded to a stop in the gravel, and Peter emerged from the driver's side.

He left the car idling, and, as he crossed in front of the headlight beams, I saw that his shirt was ripped in several places, and he was disheveled, a far cry from his usual dapper self. And he was all smiles.

"What the hell happened to you?" Rachel asked. "You left us trapped in that pit."

"Well, as you can see, I got into a bit of a scuffle."

He said he intended to find help immediately, but on the way to Ma's car, a fierce, crazy dog came out from behind the cabin and jumped him. He had to fight it off with his bare hands and was never so scared in his life. He showed us the actual rips in his shirt torn by the dog's claws.

He thought he was a goner for sure, until he managed to stun the beast with a fast kick to his snout, which gave him enough time to open the car door and dive in. But the dog didn't give up. It charged back, and Peter was lucky to slam the door shut before the beast took a chunk out of his face.

It was terrifying. The dog barked relentlessly and kept banging against his car door and pawing at the window, smearing strings of saliva on the glass. All the chaos pushed his nerves into overdrive, and he revealed how doubly dangerous that was because of his heart condition. He was never, under any circumstances to put himself in such stressful situations and exert himself the way he had. Doctor's orders.

He lowered his voice to a whisper. "Please don't share this intimacy with Mrs. Winter. My condition is very serious, and she'd worry."

He said that the dog must have lost interest and slunk away. Peter sat there the better part of an hour to calm down, and only when his heartbeat returned to normal, did he dare drive back to the barn where he swapped her car with his own, since he had more gas. It took forever, because it was dark, and the route was filled with dips and bumps. Every time the car bounced, he was jostled horribly and had to stop and rest, for fear his heart would become over-excited again.

"Can you imagine anything so frightful?"

"Yes, we can," Rachel said from her spot on the grass. "It was much worse for us. You left us down in a dark pit with two dead bodies!"

"Maybe that was worse for you, but at least they were dead. The creature I had to contend with was very much alive!"

Peter's story would have been otherwise unbelievable, had it not jived with Tornado's version of the dog at the cabin. "Well, so what are you doing here, n-n-now?" I asked.

"What do you mean? I've been driving around ever since, trying to find someone to help you. I guess I'm not needed now."

"Are you kidding? You have a car, and we need to go to town, any town."

"Well, I suppose I could. I should probably tell Mrs. Winter that I'm taking you, though."

"No, you can't tell her!" My flare-up startled him. But we couldn't let him see either the kitchen or Ma tied up. We insisted that Rachel had to see a doctor right away, and I convinced him that all he needed to do was drop us off. I started to lift Rachel into the back seat on my own, grateful it would be the last time for a while, and I looked to him for assistance.

"Oh, I'm sorry, I can't," he said, placing his hand on his chest. "My heart, remember?"

I convinced him to swing by the crashed car to pick up our gear where we'd left it scattered on the grass. Peter was aghast at the wreckage, and Rachel did her best to describe how the accident transpired.

"If you don't mind, we'll take the front gate this time," he said, with a nervous giggle. "It'll be less dramatic than trying to smash through."

"That's very nice of you, Peter," Rachel said, "but unless your car has wings and can fly over Ma's fence, we're stuck until she opens the gate. We've been trying to get out of here for ages."

He snickered again. "Heavens, wings won't be necessary. I have a key. She gave me one years ago, right after Pa died."

Thrilled to catch a break at last, I made quick work of tossing our gear into his trunk. I hopped in the back with Rachel and asked him if we might drive by the compost heap to pick up the last of the hikers. He was small and wouldn't take up much room. Maybe he could ride in the front.

"I hope you're not speaking of the one they call Sparky. His smell is quite repellent, and I couldn't abide him stinking up my car. In any case, I thought you said you were in a hurry."

When I protested, he convinced me there simply was not enough time. He was happy to help Rachel and me to make up for stranding us up earlier, but he hoped we understood he was under no obligation to assist anyone else. I appreciated his generosity and slipped off my watch. It was the only valuable I had left, and I remembered he'd admired it. I offered it to him for all his kindness.

"Oh, no, I couldn't," he said, waving it away.

"Please, take it. You have no idea how g-g-grateful we are."

Reluctantly, he slid it on his wrist. "You know, I did have a customer in mind who was asking for a nice piece like this, but I can hardly sell a gift, can I? Now that I see it up close, I believe I'll keep it for myself."

I felt smug as we drove up the driveway past the house, with the headlights on high beam. Even if Ma saw us go by, I knew she wouldn't be able to do a thing about it. I made a grand gesture of giving her the finger as we passed. A few moments later as we neared the gate, Rachel squirmed in her seat.

"I think I'm going to be sick," she gurgled. "Yes, I'm positive."

"Oh, dear!" Peter groaned. With only twenty feet left to go, he slammed on the brakes. Springing from the car, he yanked her out and dragged her several yards away on the grass.

"I apologize for all the drama, but the thought of vomit in the back seat was indeed nauseating. I can't imagine how I would ever get the smell out." He clutched his chest. "I'm sorry, but all this is making me anxious, and I was already feeling a little off as it is. For your sake, I hope it doesn't mean we'll have to turn around and go back, so I can recoup."

Go back? I panicked at the thought that we wouldn't follow through with the escape. "What can I d-d-do to help?" I asked.

"Maybe while your friend is over there doing her business, you would do me the favor of opening the gate for us? I'm wearing a pacemaker, and they tell me that even a small current could cause it to explode."

"Don't worry. We made sure to turn off the power on the way out."

"That was smart. Between you and me, sometimes I don't think Mrs. Winter realizes how dangerous that fence can be, and I fear she can be a little reckless with it."

He handed me a single, old-fashioned key and asked me to unlock it for him. I wasted no time and rushed to the gate. While I hated leaving Rachel alone, I wasn't willing to let his condition screw up our escape. We were so close.

I followed his instructions and found the lock nestled in a thick coat of rubber, no doubt used as a safety measure. When I turned the key, the gate started to roll open. When it was wide enough for the car to pass through, he gave me the signal to turn it off. I turned the key back, and the gate stopped. Peter pressed on the gas and drove through. When the car was safely on the other side, he got out.

"Why don't you go back and get your friend now, if she's finished being sick? And, please, hurry."

"Two s-s-seconds," I said, tossing him the key. I chuckled that he actually caught it. Maybe I'd be able to laugh again after all. My endless ordeal was over. I rushed to pick up Rachel, and her smile told me she could sense freedom, too. I slung one of her arms over my shoulders.

Only twenty more feet to go, I thought, as I lumbered along. We were almost there.

The sudden and repeated blares and flashing red lights of a warning alarm caught me by surprise. The blare was followed by the loud clanking of metal cogs engaging with chains, as the workings of the front gate started to slide shut. I hustled as fast as I could, but Rachel's weight dragged me like an anchor.

"Hey, hold it open! We're coming as fast as we can."

But the door was faster. With only five feet to go, we watched in dread as it slammed shut, and the locking mechanism fell into place.

"Oh, my. It seems you're too late," Peter said as if it were nothing.

He held the key in his fingers and appeared more amused than apologetic. I begged him to open it again, but he refused, suggesting the exertion might do him in.

"You're joking, right?" I had just watched him jump out of the car and haul Rachel ten yards, and he didn't appear to be bothered by that exertion. I offered to do all the work and reminded him he couldn't leave with our things in his trunk.

"Thanks for reminding me," he sneered. "They will bring a nice price at my shop. And with the holiday weekend coming up, I can even raise my prices."

I knew then Peter never intended to take us to town, and I accused him of being in on everything with Ma.

"Whatever gave you that idea? I don't want you with me, because I fear the association. Ma told me you were trouble. Something about you and the girl murdering someone, or was it a couple of people? It sounded so preposterous, I wasn't sure whether to believe her. Frankly, though, I can't get involved. As a pillar of the community, I've got my reputation to maintain."

"Yeah well, not for long. Your days are n-n-numbered and so are hers. I'm not sure just how, but believe me, you're both going to pay. As a matter of fact, she's tied up in her own storeroom right now. We were going to leave her there, but now I've got a better idea."

Peter's laugh was dark and chilling. "As if she can't get herself out of a hogtie. We used to make a game of it when we were kids. She was a regular Houdini. But enough about her. I really must be going."

He slammed his car door and floored it, burning rubber as he sped away.

"So much for his condition," I moaned. "D-D-Damn it all. I knew there was something far-fetched about the dog attack. Like Peter would ever do hand-to-hand combat."

Rachel took some of the blame and said she noticed something odd about the rips in his shirt. They were too precise, as though made by scissors and not vicious claws. And where were the blood and the scratch marks? If she had more of her wits about her, she would have challenged him.

"What good would that have done?"

"Probably nothing," she groaned. "No wonder Ma didn't resist when I tied her up. She knew she wouldn't be there long. But how did he know I put her in a hogtie?"

"Now we know he was playing us the whole time." I shook my head. "And with her untied, we've got that m-m-maniac to worry about again. Is it only me or are things getting worse by the minute?"

An opossum scurried out of the woods. It was fat and pale and it hissed at us before bounding away toward the fence. *Zap!* It twitched a few times, and then its fur burst into flames as electric current pulsed through its grotesque body.

"Yeah, things are getting worse," she grumbled. "It looks like Ma turned the fence back on."

22

"We're trapped!" Rachel screamed in frustration and smashed her fist into the tree she was leaning against. When she pulled her hand back, her knuckles were bleeding, and she shook it out, wincing. "Why can't we ever catch a break?"

From her haggard face, it was clear she was still exhausted from hauling Red all the way to the farmhouse after our accident. Her ankle throbbed angrily inside Sparky's sock, which was now tight for the engorged mass that used to resemble her foot, and now her hand hurt, too.

I understood why she was in a foul mood. We both were, but I couldn't remember the last time she lost her cool like that. I also couldn't remember when we ate last, and I realized I was ravenous. Maybe that was it. Adrenaline had been masking my own hunger, and I knew she had to be starving, too.

Still, her recent erratic behavior disturbed me. Rachel had always been the level-headed one who kept us moving forward, and I worried that if she was starting to crack, we were in serious trouble. I asked if she was okay.

"I guess. I lost control there for a minute."

"Yeah, who wouldn't after what we've been through? Just don't hurt yourself again. You're banged up enough."

She sucked on her bruises. "Strider, how are we ever going to get out of here? We've tried everything. We'll never go through the fence, and we certainly can't go over."

Light bulb. If we couldn't go through or over, then we'd have to go under. We could dig a tunnel! I didn't understand why it took me so long to come up with an idea that had been staring me in the face. For days now, all I'd done was dig. I was good at it, and I'd gotten fast. Tunneling out would be sweet revenge and doubly fun, because it would be like Ma had trained me to escape. I'd beat her at her own game, and she had paid me for my trouble.

As good as I was at digging, I was sleep-deprived and knew I couldn't do it alone. When I told Rachel the plan, she wanted to pitch in, but it was out of the question. In her state, she'd end up requiring more help than any work she might contribute.

I wondered if I could lean on Sparky for another favor, and there was only one way to find out. I wished I had something to give him, but since Peter had my watch, I didn't have anything of value left. I hoped his freedom would be enough.

In the meantime, I had to figure out a way to transport Rachel to the garden. She could no longer walk, and I couldn't afford to spend energy carrying her. I was drained myself, and if I was going to be digging a tunnel, I needed every ounce of strength I could muster.

And then, I got lucky. Sticking out of some nearby brush, behind the tree Rachel pounded earlier, were the handles of a wheelbarrow, and how I ever picked it out in the dark was a miracle.

When I moved in for closer inspection, I wasn't disappointed. It was quite the relic, covered with dirt and rust, and the tire was flat, but the tub was deep and would do the trick.

I knew it was going to be a very uncomfortable ride. We couldn't risk being seen by taking the relatively smooth driveway that passed in front of the farmhouse, so I planned to sneak back behind a string of bushes that lined a side field.

The terrain would be rough and uneven, and without a rubber tire to absorb the shock, the front metal wheel would hit every dip. There would be plenty of them, and I knew her ride would be excruciating.

"Your chariot awaits," I said, helping her settle in. "Get comfortable, it's the best we've got. If for some reason we hit a bump, you can't make any noise. We don't want to alert Ma to what we're doing."

The trek to the garden was rough on both of us, the terrain only partly to blame. The wheelbarrow itself was ancient, the tub was cast iron and the frame and handles made of heavy oak, so even empty it weighed a ton. The lack of a functioning tire made the journey backbreaking and required Herculean effort.

As I trudged over the rugged terrain, I tried to steer clear of bumps, but in the dark they were nearly impossible to avoid, so not only did her ankle scream every inch of the way, her tailbone suffered as well.

Sparky greeted us when we got there. He'd planted the dill seeds for Daisy's bed, and he was so excited, he couldn't keep his voice down. Rachel tried to quiet him, warning that Ma might hear and figure out where we were.

He didn't follow. "So, what if she does?"

We couldn't believe how clueless he was. Didn't he know she was trying to kill us? Once she learned we were out there, she would be after us in a heartbeat. I got right to the point and said I wanted to dig a tunnel, and I asked him for his help. Unexpectedly, he said it sounded like fun, and he ran to pick up shovels.

"Three?" Rachel asked, when she saw the small collection he brought. "I don't think I'll be doing much digging this time." She pointed to her foot. "Can you believe how bad this looks?"

"I can give you my other sock," he said, pulling off his boot.

"No, I meant my foot looked bad, not your sock."

Sparky said he brought an extra shovel in case she changed her mind, because it would be a long way to come back for one if she did. When I asked him where he thought we would dig, he gestured to the other side of the house. But I pointed to the fence that loomed nearest to the garden and asked why we wouldn't dig there. He shook his head and said the ground was too hard and would be much softer where the fence ran down by the pond. It sounded better to me for another reason. It was farther from the house, and Ma wouldn't likely see us at work.

We were about to leave when I noticed Rachel was trembling. "Wh-Wh-What's with the shaking? Are you scared?"

"No, I'm just frazzled by the ride back. I hate to be such a pain, but can I stay here and rest while you guys dig the tunnel? You can come for me when you're done."

I knew it was an awful idea. At any moment, Ma could come out of the house and do God knows what to her. On the other hand, I was struck by how crappy she looked. There were deep purple bruises under her eyes and her skin had turned a clammy yellow. And she reeked.

In spite of the powerful alkalinity of Ma's soap and water, her smell overpowered me. If I hadn't recently been sloshing around with scrub brushes and mops, I imagined I'd smell like the odor of a thousand corpses, too, and my clothes probably did. I agreed with her. If she didn't rest and regain some strength, the final passage would be harder on the rest of us.

I carried her across the garden and laid her alongside Red's grave, behind the mound. It wasn't much of a hiding space, but I banked on Ma not noticing her from a distance.

Rachel smiled gratefully and closed her eyes. She was asleep before we left.

Sparky didn't stop talking for the entire walk to the fence, but I mostly didn't pay attention. I was careful to engage now and then because I didn't want to risk insulting him, since I needed his help. From time to time I caught a few snippets like "careful of them copperheads" and something about the compost, but I was so lost in thought I paid little attention to the context.

He stopped me at a part of the fence close to the water and pointed to a spot on the ground. I was thrilled when I stabbed my shovel into the patch of dirt and it pierced through to the hilt without much effort.

"Told you," he said, giving me a high-five.

While the shovel went in easily, the loads were heavy, and digging was more tiring than I expected. He plugged along beside me, but he wasn't much of a digger and he only dug half as fast. He never stopped talking, either, which was undoubtedly why Ma put him on compost duty and not with other hikers.

After we got down about two feet deep, I hit a snag. Because we couldn't let our metal shovels touch the fence, we couldn't tell when to stop digging down and start digging under. I knew the fence didn't stop at the grass line and was set below ground. I just didn't know how deep.

"Oh, it goes down pretty far," Sparky said, when I asked. "Ma told me Pa staked it in deep to keep out the critters. You ever seen how they can dig under a fence?"

"Wait a minute. How far down?"

"In some places I think it goes down at least five."

Five feet? That stark revelation made my head throb, and it hurt even more than my aching back. It was inconceivable anyone would set a fence that deep into the ground, but it was

168

all I had to go on so, like my name, I took it in stride and continued to dig.

It was slow going, particularly since Sparky was not very helpful. I kept thinking how much faster it would have been if Red was there to help. With the extra hand, we'd have finished and been out. At three feet deep, I signaled that I needed a break.

Rachel

While she was grateful to be lying on her back, her ankle ached more than ever and contributed to her fitful sleep. She woke with a pounding headache and knew what that meant. She wished she could tell Strider what was wrong, but he had enough on his mind, and she didn't want to complicate their relationship further. After they were safely out of the farm, she planned to level with him. By then they'd be happy together again, and he'd be more open-minded.

She dozed off, and before long she was deep in a dream. She was lying on the table in Ma's kitchen listening to someone banging on the door from inside the storeroom. Then, she saw dirt blowing out from under the door.

The banging stopped and was replaced by a heaving sound from the wooden door that began to pulse like a membrane. Soon massive amounts of dirt spewed out from the under of the door and swirled up to the ceiling, where it formed a cloud and sprinkled down on her like soft rain.

While the light dusting of dirt felt almost pleasant, she knew if she didn't leave the room the dirt would eventually fill her nose and mouth and she'd suffocate. But she couldn't leave. She was stuck to the table and couldn't stand up.

Bam! The storeroom door blew open and slammed into the wall. This time the dirt that fell on her face was coarse and heavy.

Rachel gasped for breath. Her eyes shot open and she clutched her throat. When she saw that she was still lying outside on the ground where Strider had left her, she closed her eyes again, relieved it was only a nightmare.

Until she felt dirt strike her face again. This time it was real, and she raised herself up on one arm to see where it was coming from. The sky was dark and the night so still that for a moment, what she saw made her believe she was still in the dream.

A finger sticking out from Red's grave flicked up and down at the surface, sending dirt in her direction. The rest of the topsoil was pulsating, too, not moving up and down so much as shifting outward from the center.

When she leaned over, a hand shot out and clawed at her. She screamed at the top of her lungs and lurched back, dead certain she was awake. She watched in disbelief as the hand grabbed at the ground beside her.

All at once, Red shot up from the garden bed. "Pfft!" He spat dirt from his mouth and brushed himself off.

"Red?!" she gasped. "You're alive!"

He turned his bandaged body toward her. "Yes, and I could use a drink of water."

23

I was tired and discouraged. I felt like we'd been digging forever, but I wasn't convinced we were making much progress. Sparky was taking his tenth "water break" and winding down another of his endless stories, when he asked me if I thought we could actually dig all the way to China.

"I don't know, Sparky, if we don't start digging under the fence pretty soon, we may end up there. I wish there was a way we could tell if we've cleared it. I don't want to touch it with my shovel and find out the hard way."

"Wait! We're digging a tunnel *under* the fence?"

"Where else?" I said, wondering how he could be so dense.

"Well, why didn't you say so? Offhand, I'd say we're down plenty deep to dig under, but I'll check."

I wasn't comfortable with Sparky as the guinea pig, but I changed my mind. He had become more of an annoyance than a help, and I was desperate, so I didn't object. By now the hole was so deep that when Sparky jumped in, his head was barely above ground level.

"Yeah, we're good to go," he shouted. "Looks like we dug down deeper than we had to, ha-ha. Maybe by three or four feet. Should I start digging under the fence now?"

I was infuriated. "You told me the bottom of the fence went down five feet!"

"Five feet? No, why would I? See? Sometimes, I don't think you listen to anything I say. Maybe five *inches*. Who in their right mind would set a fence in five feet?"

I cursed him and my bad luck for wasting so much of our precious time on unnecessary and backbreaking labor. We could have been out by then. Besides, I was almost certain he'd said five feet. On the other hand, he was right. I was so used to ignoring him, I easily could have tuned him out or heard him wrong. But I understood why he volunteered to check the clearance.

We began implementing a system I'd seen prisoners use to escape in the movies. The person below would dig and fill their pail with the dirt. Then he handed it up to the guy on top, who would empty it and send it back down.

When Sparky was doing the digging, we didn't make as much headway, but it gave me a breather and a rest for my over-taxed muscles. At least we were headed in the right direction—out! Going up on the other side would be easier, too, I figured, because we would have the advantage of gravity. Instead of lifting a shovel full of dirt, all we would need to do going forward was pick at it, and the dirt would fall down on its own. We'd be out in two hours.

I was working the above-ground shift when I heard Rachel's voice. I knew she couldn't have made it on her own and wondered how she got there.

"Guys! Look who came back from the dead to help us!"

The first thing I saw was her legs dangling out of the wheelbarrow, and when she came into focus, I was astonished to see Red behind it, pushing her as if it were child's play. He still had dozens of tiny cuts everywhere, and several shards of windshield we must have missed stuck out of his face. He was caked with dirt, and he struck me more like a horror film zombie than my hiker friend. At least he was quite alive.

Hearing the commotion, Sparky stuck his head out of the hole. "Hey, where did you find that wheelbarrow? It's been missing for ages."

172

"What the hell, Sparky? Don't you even recognize the guy you just buried alive!"

"Oh, sorry. Hey, don't hold it against me, will you? Strider told me to bury you, so I did."

I wiped away a tear with my dirty sleeve and ran over to put my arm around Red, careful not to aggravate his wounds. After seeing all the dead hikers, I was overjoyed to find my friend was no longer one of them.

The first thing I did was assure him that Sparky's version was not how it actually transpired. Red laughed and said his experience reminded him of the scene in *The Princess Bride* when Miracle Max and his wife Valerie pronounce Westly only "mostly dead." Like the hero in the movie, Red was alive enough to pull through.

"You should have seen Rachel's face when I sat straight up in my grave."

He didn't remember much after they rammed into the fence, but he assumed he'd blacked out or fallen into a coma. He figured his breathing was probably so shallow, Sparky didn't think he was breathing at all.

"In a weird way, being buried alive might have actually saved my life, because it gave my body a chance to rejuvenate."

Barely alive was more like it, I thought, as I scanned his distressed body. Thanks to Rachel's bandages, it appeared his bleeding had stopped, and before they left to meet up with Sparky and me, she retied a few. Red was definitely a walking marvel. The most miraculous thing was, that after all that he been through, the large piece of glass was still firmly lodged in his shoulder.

"Rachel said you guys were tunneling out, and I knew if she had to count on you to do the digging, you'd never make it," he joked. "But digging by the pond? I can't imagine how heavy the ground is because of the water."

"Yeah, it was Sparky's idea, and you're right, every shovelful weighs a ton."

"Hey, don't blame it on me," Sparky said from below. "I said it was softer, not easier. You're the one who got mixed up and dug down too far."

After I cleared up the misunderstanding about the depth, Red held up a hand. "Five feet, five inches. It's not important now. Let's get going. We have digging to do."

Though he assured me he felt fine, I was unconvinced. But it was apparent that I couldn't prevent him from pitching in. He grabbed a shovel and put himself in rotation with me. The two of us took turns tunneling, and Sparky remained permanently in the position emptying the pail above ground. Working side by side with Red elevated my spirits and gave me a second wind.

It also gave me time to fill him in about what happened while he was underground. I couldn't help but tell him the truth about everything that happened, even Daisy's death. I trusted my friend to understand my point of view, and it was a relief to be off my chest.

"Good thing you didn't get out, after all," he laughed, when he heard about Peter's betrayal at the gate. "Or I'd be left here with that maniac woman."

It wasn't long before he announced we could start to tunnel up. At the current rate, he guessed we'd be done in an hour, but I was afraid that was being optimistic. I'd been keeping an eye on him when we switched jobs and noted that it took him longer to pull himself out of the hole each time. But he powered on, though it was often a struggle just to catch his breath. When he asked to rest a minute, I panicked.

"Hey, I'm fine. I wanted to stop, because I need to tell you something." He struggled to get out the words. "And I'll make it fast. I never came on to Dani. I know I told you that before, but I need you to believe I was telling you the truth then. I'm a good guy."

I regretted that he and I hadn't met elsewhere. Under different circumstances we might have been great friends. "What the heck, of course you are. You're the best. Don't worry, I do believe you." I pointed at Rachel who was dozing off in the wheelbarrow. "And I have a question for you, too. You warned me to watch out for her. What was that about?"

He frowned. "Oh, gosh. The two of you seem so close now, I'd hate to say anything that might muddy the waters."

"It's not as rosy as you think."

"Well, at least that will make it easier when you get back in touch with CutePuppy124."

I stood up. "Holy crap! I can't believe I forgot to tell you. Guess what? CutePuppy124 is Rachel!"

Red's eyes nearly popped out of his head. "No way! Then, I guess I should tell you something. While you were in Harpers Ferry, she was all over me, begging me to have sex with her. I turned her down, but she had trouble taking no for an answer. I didn't tell you before, because between Daisy and CutePuppy124, I knew you were feeling vulnerable. Funny how that worked out, isn't it?"

"Yeah, it's weird," I whispered. "She told me the opposite, that you came onto her. Why do you think she lied?"

Red shrugged. "Who knows? Maybe she was afraid I would tell you first. The important thing now is that I want you to trust me."

"All right. I do, okay?"

"Thanks. Now enough about that stupid stuff. If we're getting out of here, we've got to keep going."

"Stop saying, *we*. I've been watching you, and I don't think you're in any condition to continue digging. You're short of breath, and you look like death warmed over."

"I *am* death warmed over, remember?" He admitted that a couple of his cuts were bleeding again, but it was no big deal. He pushed me aside to grab his shovel. This time when he got up, I saw the back of his pants were soaked. He was pale, and he swayed side to side.

"Red, is that sweat? Slow down and give yourself a break, will you?"

"I'm fine, okay?"

I wanted to force him to rest, but I had to face facts. I was desperate. Sparky had wandered off, and there was no way I could finish the tunnel by myself. It took everything I had in me to dig down far, and I needed all the help I could get.

Red was about to climb down into the hole when, without warning, he crumpled to the ground.

"Are you all right?" I rushed over, and even in the dark I could tell the wetness on his pants was not sweat, but blood. "What's wrong with you? Why didn't you tell me you were bleeding? We could have done something."

He was panting hard and couldn't speak.

"Stay with us, okay? I'm going to find something to stop the bleeding."

"Forget it, Strider. You can't do anything for me. I think I dug myself to death. I wish I could help, but getting out is up to you, now."

"Don't talk crazy, Red. After all we've been through, I'm not letting you die."

"Why not?" Rachel whispered, from a few feet away. She sounded defeated. "We're all going to die here because of that damned fence. The only time we had a chance to escape was when Tornado's body shorted the power. We could have climbed it then, but we were too stupid to realize it."

"Then use me," Red murmured.

His voice was so soft I wasn't certain I'd heard him correctly.

"Use me to short out the fence, like Tornado did. She's right, I'm not going to last long. I've lost a ton of blood, and it's not like you guys can give me a transfusion."

I was horrified. "Christ. I can't do that."

"We don't have a choice," Rachel said quietly. "He's right about dying, just look at him. I don't know how long my little bandages will hold. I'm not a nurse, you know."

She had a point. Red wouldn't last another hour.

"I'm not throwing him at the fence, but I'm not going to stand here and watch him die, either!" I ripped off my filthy t-shirt to make a tourniquet for his leg.

Red smiled. "Hey buddy, do me a favor, will you?"

"Anything. Just ask."

He complained that the chunk of windshield stuck in his shoulder was starting to come loose and asked if I would hold onto it for a second, so he could make a little adjustment. Though I thought the request was strange, I was happy to oblige my friend, and I gingerly pinched the end of the glass, careful not to jiggle it and cause him pain.

"Now what?"

"Hold it for another second, okay?"

Red took me by surprise and jerked backward, pulling himself free from the shard of glass. Blood spurted from the gash, some of it splashing in my eye. I wiped it away in time to see his eyes flicker and blood drip down his bare arms and chest. I was still holding the bloody chunk of glass in my fingers.

"What the hell did you do that for?"

"You weren't going to do what I asked while I was alive. My life's over now. Throw me against the fence to short it out, and then use me for a ladder."

"No, man. I can't do that. Come on, you'll make it."

"I'm bleeding out, and you know it. Use me, you idiot. You've got no alternative." He kept smiling, even as his voice got weaker. "And don't be stupid and touch me once I'm against the fence. You need to stay alive to report this place to the police."

His voice was barely audible. "Oh, and my real name is Christopher. I thought someone should know."

Red's head dropped to his chest, and I cried when I saw my friend exhale for the final time. I was still holding the piece of glass in my fingers when I heard the familiar voice.

"So." It was Ma, sitting in a golf cart right behind me. "Are you trying to kill all my hikers?"

24

"You seem to be doing a pretty good job at killing them, yourself," I said.

"Easier than paying them." She sighed. "Do you have any idea how hard it is to keep a small farm afloat? Of course, you don't. Maybe I should throw some light on it for you."

She told me that it was hard enough to keep their farm in the black even when Pa was alive. It took nonstop work, and they were younger then, strong and capable. After Pa died, she had to hire several workers just to replace him, and she could see the writing on the wall. Making ends meet was going to be next to impossible. Until she came up with the arrangement with the hikers.

Ma got the idea when she heard that many hikers were often short of cash by the time they reached Harpers Ferry, and that they frequently sought temporary work there. So, she posted flyers as an experiment to attract part-time help, and when the phone started to ring off the wall, she knew she was onto something.

With the proper instruction, she found that hikers could successfully plow, plant, fertilize and harvest her crops. It was a chance for them to make some easy money with no strings attached, and she didn't have to pay them as much as regular farmhands. Letting them camp on her property encouraged them to work longer and cost her practically nothing.

Due partly to her winning personality and the notorious fun and camaraderie of the campfire at the end of a workday, word of mouth spread up and down the trail. And with the additional help of Peter's advocacy with hikers wandering into the Lost and Found, before long the farm had a consistent workforce.

While the cheaper labor put Winter's Farm in the black again, the setup was still pricier than she liked, and she looked for another way to cut costs. During those nights around the campfire, she learned something else as she chatted up her guests. More than a few had taken to the trail because they were loners. Others left bad relationships or dropped out of society temporarily, while they turned their lives around. It didn't take long for her to experiment with a system that would give her the manpower she needed without the cost.

It was risky, and she started slowly, testing it out first on hikers who wouldn't be missed. On payday, she made a grand gesture of doling out cash to everybody at the same time, but she recouped much of that outflow by ensuring that hikers who planned to leave after being paid "left a little early."

It was a big farm, which made it easy to dispose of their bodies and gear in creative ways. She'd take back what she paid them and bonus herself with what she found in their backpacks and pockets. Then she'd recycle it again by pretending to pay the next hiker.

To encourage them to work longer, she sometimes offered to pay double or triple, and it was nearly impossible to resist the intoxicating amounts of money she'd offer. Thanks to the other arrangement she made with Peter and the Lost and Found, she could even fence their valuables. He never asked questions, and since the hikers she'd select had few or no family ties, nobody else asked questions, either.

Ma didn't kill all the hikers who worked for her. She made sure that enough got back to the trail to talk up Winter's Farm as the "go-to" place for temporary work, and Ma as the fun and generous hostess. She knew it was necessary, but still, she hated parting with the cash.

I was appalled at what she was saying. "You're a disgusting human being, and I use the term loosely. I'm glad I'll be the one to take you down."

"You're out of your league. And who have you got left to help you? That psycho whore?"

"Don't you call me that, bitch!" Rachel struggled to her feet, but I restrained her.

"Take your hands off me!" She tried to wrest herself away, but her leg couldn't support the rest of her, and she fell down, shrieking from pain.

I attempted to grab her again, but she screamed at me, "I said, don't touch me!"

"Why are you yelling at me? Why don't you rest for a few minutes? You're just tired."

"Don't tell me what I am!" She wriggled free again. "Leave me alone!"

With everything she'd been through, her moodiness was understandable, and I was willing to let it slide. "She's not herself at the moment," I explained, though I had to admit I was concerned.

"Not herself, my ass. That's exactly who she is. That girl is cuckoo."

"She'll be fine in a few minutes. And then the two of us are going to take you down."

"Oh, yeah. You and Rachel. Great team you've got. I swear you sound dumber and dumber every time you open your mouth. That girl's not fine. She's a wreck, because she's off her meds. Or didn't you know that, either?"

"Off what meds? Are you trying to mess with my head again?"

"Ha. Don't have to. Seeing is believing. I watched her pop pills all day long back in my kitchen. Every day, every four hours. Took a gander at the labels to find out what she was taking once, too, when I had the chance. Land sakes, I couldn't pronounce them long names. Psycho may not be strong enough to describe that mess of a child."

"Is this true, Rachel?" I asked her sweetly. "Are you all right? Can I get you something?"

"Screw you!" she snapped. Her eyes fluttered briefly, and then she withdrew and became quiet.

Ma chuckled. "See what I mean? Peter said he found the pills in her backpack and asked if he should run back with them. I told him she wouldn't need them anymore. Or, should I say Melody won't need them anymore, as it says on the prescription bottle."

Melody? So, Rachel lied to me about her name, too? What was I doing that attracted these people? I remembered what she told me the night we were out searching for Daisy: "I'm just plain Rachel." A blatant lie. And there was that other offhand comment she made when we discovered Daisy's inhaler in the cabin. She said something about knowing what it was like to be without medication. Of course, it didn't register with me at the time.

Rachel's mood swings had become more frequent, and I was beginning to doubt that stress and fatigue were the only reasons behind them. Maybe Ma was right, and it had to do with medication.

She became docile again and let me pull her close, but she didn't respond when I questioned her. She seemed to understand me but was unable to answer.

"See what you've done?" I was furious. "You've made her so anxious, she can barely talk."

"She can't speak because she's off her rocker, you dope. What more proof do you need? Anyway, I don't know why you hate me so much, I'm not the one that tied up your girlfriend."

"What are you talking about?! Then who did?"

She let out a belly laugh and turned to Rachel. "Do you want to tell him, or should I?"

I saw Rachel's eyes shoot wide open.

Ma continued to badger. "Yeah, that slut you've been shacking up with did it. She stole the key to my storeroom and dumped your girlfriend in there when I was out meditating."

I jumped to Rachel's defense. "Now you're the one who's talking crazy. How could Daisy have been in there the whole time without you knowing?"

"Who said I didn't know? I might be a little deaf, but I'm not dumb."

Ma thought she could convince me that Rachel had kidnapped Daisy. I trusted Rachel more than anyone else at the farm and was sure Ma was just trying to rattle me. "Give me a break."

She shrugged. "Believe what you want. Isn't it obvious? She wanted to get Daisy out of the picture, so she could have you all to herself. Ha! And you were so stupid, you fell for it. Go ahead, ask her."

I wanted Rachel to tell me she was innocent. "Rachel, is this true?" I didn't think there was anything left in the world that would make me feel worse than I already felt, but when I saw her nod and admit her guilt, she repulsed me.

"I can explain," she cried.

"I'm sure you can," I replied with tears in my eyes.

"Ha-ha. There you go again, crying like a baby," Man teased. "Go ahead, put her out of her misery. I've seen you murder before."

"I hate you." Then I turned to Rachel. "I hate you both!"

Ma's golf cart beeped loudly when she switched it to reverse. "I'll tell you what I hate. I hate the sound this dern thing makes when I back up. Is there anything more tiresome?"

25

As I watched her sitting smugly on her golf cart, I realized that in addition to everything else that revolted me about her, now I even hated the sound of Ma's voice. Nevertheless, her comment about my being a murderer stung.

Murder wasn't the right word. Perhaps I was splitting hairs. In my mind, I hadn't murdered anyone. Killed, maybe. There was Daisy, and I still tried to convince myself it was an accident. And, if Ma was to be believed and Daisy was pregnant, I'd have to count her baby as part of the same accident. In any case, I'd never know now.

I hadn't technically killed Tornado, either, but I knew a case could be made that she wouldn't have been in that predicament if hadn't been for me. Ditto for Red, although I did feel responsible for the accident, and I had pulled the glass from his arm. I tried to search for the right term to describe my involvement. Involuntary manslaughter? Yes, that was what they called it. But maybe in Red's case, they'd call it suicide.

But for all my excuses, I couldn't help the sinking feeling settled in my gut. Accident or not, people were dead as a result of my actions, and I wasn't sure if I could ever forgive myself.

"Daisy was wrong for you. You and I were meant for each other," Rachel wailed out of the blue. "You know I'm right."

Was it as simple as being terrible at picking women? I'd been sharing my bed with Rachel, and now I didn't know who she was. Thinking back to when I first met CutePuppy124, I remembered making a point of not rushing things. We both did. It took forever before I agreed to speak on the phone the first time. If that wasn't being smart, what was?

Then things fell apart with her and I left town. The nagging question now was how the heck she found me at Winter's Farm.

Little did I know how easy it was to figure out. I'd led her right to me. When my friends pressed me for details about my hike, I posted my whole itinerary on social media, including the stop in Harpers Ferry. I promised I'd update everyone when I got there, but by the time I arrived I was preoccupied with my new girlfriend and forgot to check in.

26

CutePuppy124

CutePuppy124 had made a big investment in the guy who called himself Strider, and she was not about to give up on him simply because he gave up on her. She had no idea how long it would take to find him, and she withdrew a substantial amount of money from her savings to finance her mission. She called into work complaining of a terrible stomach virus, which allowed her to use sick days to make the initial trip to Harpers Ferry.

She was lucky she didn't have to use her real name when she checked into the hostel. It turned out most of the hikers registered with their trail names and not their legal ones. She registered as Rachel, a name pulled from thin air, because she feared complications at her office should they discover she had not been ill after all. As an extra measure of discretion, she paid cash in advance for several nights.

The first day she systematically crisscrossed the town, identifying places where hikers were known to congregate. Then, she drew a route on a street map and followed it religiously in a loop several times a day to be certain she wouldn't miss him. Her mobile phone was loaded with photos he'd sent her when they were actively an item, and during her rare breaks for food and water, she flipped through them tirelessly.

When, after four days Strider still hadn't shown up, Rachel revisited the Appalachian Trail Conservancy Visitor Center to double check their maps. With the assistance of the same docent who helped her with the very same problem earlier, she recalculated the distance and the estimated hiking time between where he likely entered the trail and the town. He was due at any moment.

She became so completely immersed in her project and in being Rachel that when she placed another call to her office to authorize the use of her remaining personal days, she confused the Human Resources Department.

"Who did you say was calling, again?" the woman asked.

"Rachel. This is Rachel, you know, from billing." She was short with the director, and, after realizing her error, she scrambled to invent a plausible explanation for her curious behavior.

She ended each evening at The Tankard, the bar most frequented by hikers. Drinks were reasonable, and so was the food, and there was often a lively group at the bar. Despite the crowd, it didn't take long for the bartender to get to know her.

On her second night, he recognized her as the attractive and spunky, young woman who had drunk alone the night before, and he made the mistake of taking her home after the bar closed. While the sex was playful at first, he regretted picking her up when she became overly aggressive and borderline angry. He was uneasy when she insisted on staying the night, and the next morning when she woke up sullen and cranky, he couldn't wait for her to leave.

The experience didn't stop her from showing up at the same bar every night afterward. She was always perky and smiled, as if nothing had happened. The bartender ignored her as best he could, only transacting her drink orders. She'd weirded him out enough earlier, but she was making things worse. She was obsessed with some guy, and she badgered him to check out a couple of photographs she'd shown him twice before.

One night as she sat alone and depressed, her posture reflecting both her mood and her drink tab, the bartender tapped her shoulder and pointed to a table on the other side of the restaurant. Strider. There he was. She was ecstatic. Until she saw that he was sharing his table with another woman. From then on, she couldn't take her eyes off them.

At first, she was confused. He'd never told her he had a sister. Didn't he say he was an only child? The two of them started laughing, and Rachel felt a tinge of jealousy, wishing she was part of the fun. When they took bites out of the same burger, she got suspicious. But, then, after the girl leaned in for a quick kiss, Rachel became outraged.

A big part of her wanted to yell his name across the room and reveal herself in the presence of the whole restaurant. She imagined that if he learned CutePuppy124 was right there in the same room, all would be forgiven. He would swoop her up and never give that slut another thought. But she had to control herself, because winning him back would take some one-on-one time, and she'd have to do it without him knowing her true identity.

She followed them out, but not before picking up a card they'd left behind on the table. *Day Workers Needed. $100 a day. Winter's Farm.*

"Do you know what this is?" she asked the server, slurring her words.

"Oh, yeah. everyone around here knows Winter's Farm. Hikers sometimes go there to work for a few days. They're going there tomorrow."

"They?" Rachel was so furious, she had trouble forming words. "Who was that woman?"

"How should I know? I assumed they were a couple."

"A couple?" she snapped. "Ha! That's impossible. He and I are the couple."

The server held up her hands. "Hey, don't shoot the messenger. All I know is they certainly acted like one. They sure loved PDA."

Rachel slammed her hands down on the table. "Are you some kind of idiot? I told you *he's with me.*"

By then, everyone in the restaurant was watching the exchange. The server backed away. "Calm down, all right? Why don't you ask them yourself?" She pointed out the window, where Strider was walking hand in hand with the other woman.

Rachel staggered back to the bar, trying to hold her head high. She threw down a couple of twenties, tossed back the rest of her drink, and stormed out.

Being in the fresh air helped clear her head, and she calmed down a little. After all, there was no way Strider could possibly be in a serious relationship so soon. He was too cautious. Still, this new woman did complicate things. She followed the couple down the street, bile rising in her throat. She knew what she had to do.

Rachel beat them to the farm the next morning, excited to use the camping gear she'd bought her first day in town. Because of the unsatisfying experience with the vanilla sex the bartender offered, Rachel was feeling antsy and thought she might have better luck with a big guy she saw working in the garden. When she found he wasn't interested, she got to work, instead.

After only a couple of hours in the garden, Ma assigned her to work in the kitchen along with the other new woman, Strider's girlfriend. Rachel despised her so much she couldn't bring herself to pronounce her name when Ma made the introductions. Instead, she was all forced smiles.

It was more than contempt. Daisy was her formal competition, so at every turn Rachel was determined to outshine her. It was easy when they were in the kitchen because she knew her way around, and Daisy didn't. Ma drove that point home when she lavished praise on Rachel for her chopping prowess and humiliated Daisy for her lack of skill.

Rachel was convinced that once Strider compared them side-by-side, he'd drop Daisy in a heartbeat and come back around to her.

But when she overheard they were engaged, she knew she had to take more drastic measures and step up her timetable. That was when she concocted her scheme to kidnap Daisy and stash her in Ma's storeroom. After all, it was only going to take a few days alone with Strider to turn him against Daisy.

Since Ma was deaf in one ear, Rachel thought she'd never notice Daisy bound and gagged in the next room. She'd seen where Ma kept the key and was sure everything would be worked out before Ma realized it was missing. By then, she had demonstrated she knew her way around the kitchen, and Ma felt comfortable leaving her in charge from time to time. Rachel used those opportunities to feed and change her captive.

27

I was repulsed when I'd heard about the sick and drastic measures Rachel had taken to win me over. I needed a moment, and I walked over to the pond to think. Then I turned back to her. "You actually thought it was okay to k-k-kidnap a pregnant woman and lock her up in a room?"

"I didn't know she was pregnant," Rachel said as she crawled over to me, no longer able to walk.

Ma laughed. "Took you long enough to figure out that one was a psycho. I knew the day she got here."

"Don't listen to her. I'm not some kind of monster," Rachel insisted. "I took really good care of Daisy, and I wasn't going to keep her there long."

"Why don't you just shut up? If it wasn't for you, sh-sh-she and I would have been out of here a long time ago. And everyone would still be alive!"

Rachel laughed. "Well, I remember your post, do you? You wrote that you had 'a couple weeks to kill' before your new job started. You sure nailed that sucker on the head."

Ma shouted from her golf cart. "Hey, tell him how you pushed Daisy into his machete on purpose, why don't you?"

I couldn't believe it. Could it be that my almost-girlfriend had murdered my almost-fiancée? I was doubly angry that Rachel allowed me to suffer with guilt for so long.

Instead of laughing now, Rachel was bawling and struggled to stand. "Don't you get it? I only wanted her out of the way, so we could be happy." She threw her arms around me. "You love me."

I pushed her away. "I can't even look at you."

"And my phone wasn't dead, either," Ma said. "She could have called the police. That screwball played you for a fool."

I ignored Ma. "Listen to yourself, Rachel. You're warped!"

"I am not *crazy*!" She lunged at me again, but I gave her shoulders a shove.

"See how you like being pushed."

She lost her balance, screamed, and tumbled backward out into the pond. It was deep, and with her feet on the mucky bottom, the water level was up to her neck.

"I can't swim!" she gasped. She splashed water chaotically in an attempt to keep upright, but it had the effect of dragging her farther away from land. "Help!" She went under.

Her foot stirred up a snake resting at the bottom, and it splashed at the surface, drawing everyone's attention. The snake made me nervous, but I couldn't bear to let her drown, so I pulled off my shoes to jump in after her.

Ma stopped me. "Don't think I'd go in if I were you. You wouldn't stand a chance against a damn copperhead."

I caught myself before I made the leap, remembering a comment Sparky made on our way to the pond. It was something about how copperheads bite more than any other venomous snake in North America.

Rachel was gasping and gulping water when her head broke the surface again. One leech had affixed itself to her cheek, and there was a second larger one on her forehead. When the snake wriggled around her neck, she screamed again. "Help me, please!"

"Dammit, I c-c-can't!" I cried.

She made a gurgling noise and then went under. I didn't see her again, until her body floated to the surface. In anger and frustration, I fell to my knees and pounded my fists on the ground.

Two snakes slithered out of the pond and glided past Ma slowly enough for her to identify them. "Well, Strider, you're about the unluckiest person I know. They were water snakes, after all, and easy to confuse. Should have known, though, we haven't seen a Copperhead around here in years."

"You b-b-bitch! I could have saved her!"

"Saved her? You're the one who threw her in!"

28

"That's five now," Ma said, as she eyeballed Rachel's floating body. "But who's counting?"

"Five what?" I asked.

"Tornado, Daisy, the baby, Red, and Rachel. That makes five people you've murdered on my farm so far. Pretty impressive, if you ask me."

With Rachel and Red gone there was no reason for me to delay any further, and I definitely wasn't in the mood for Ma's snide comments—though I had to admit she was pretty much on the mark. Sparky was still alive, but I got the feeling he was more than capable of taking care of himself.

"Don't get me started on all the people you've killed," I retorted.

Ma chuckled. "Name one."

I couldn't, of course. "It's only you and me now, Ma, and I'm a lot f-f-faster than you. Especially since you need a cane."

Her laugh was diabolical, and I was terrified by the thought she had something else up her sleeve.

"What's to s-s-stop me from leaving right now?" I asked, trying to stay calm.

"My cattle prod." She lifted her cane off the ground and gave it a playful zap in my direction. "Had it since Pa kept cows but added a few tweaks." She gave me a wink. "It comes in handy for times like these."

I shouldn't have been surprised. Almost everything I learned about her demonstrated she was more capable than she let on. She waved it in Rachel's direction.

"So, are you going to keep littering my beautiful farm with your victims? How about you pull the latest one out of my swimming hole?"

I didn't waste my breath with a comeback. "You know, I think I'll let you deal with Rachel by yourself. I'm getting the hell out of here."

I turned and walked in the direction of Red and the fence, but she blocked me off in her golf cart, forcing me back toward the edge of the pond.

"Not so fast!" she commanded.

I ignored her and kept moving. I sank lower and lower into the surrounding mush, as the mud squished and sucked at my boots, slowing me to a crawl. Soon, each footstep plunged me up to my knees, and every time I tried to move to firmer ground, she blocked my path.

I was stuck, and when I began to sink deeper, I knew I had to take drastic measures. Reaching down into the muck I untied my boots, and, with a giant leap, dove out into the pond, leaving my boots behind. I swam the short distance to the pier, and when I got out, Ma was there to meet me.

I considered my options. My socks had come off in the pond, my bare feet limited where I could run, and my soaked clothing weighed me down. I set my sights on the fence and sprinted forward, but I wasn't quick enough, and she stunned the top of one of my bare feet with her prod.

The shock was brief but powerful, and I tumbled off the pier. Luckily, I landed on dry land, but, unfortunately, she was right behind me, and she jabbed me again, this time on the other foot. The pain was searing, and my body reflexively flipped around. Now, we were face-to-face.

"There's plenty more where that came from," she blared.

My eyes grew huge as I watched the prod lunge at my groin. The shock was tortuous, and I writhed around in agony, convinced I would never walk again. Helpless, I quickly assessed my surroundings and estimated the distance to the fence at about thirty yards. Reaching it seemed an impossibility, but the vision of Red's body slumped in a heap inspired me to crawl forward on all fours.

A blistering pain tore into the back of my thigh and I cried out, collapsing to the ground. My face fell in the mud. When I reached around, I felt the pocketknife she'd thrown that was lodged up to the hinge. I crawled forward again.

"I'll teach you to underestimate Ma Winter," she hissed, zapping me on my buttocks.

"Stop! Please! I surrender." I fell back down and curled into a ball.

She laughed as she stood over me, and the prongs crackled as she pointed the prod at my head. Her eyes were wild and gleeful. "I ain't even close to done," she giggled.

She was about to zap me again when I sprang open and threw a handful of ragweed at her face.

"Take that, bitch!"

Her body twitched, and she let out an enormous sneeze, giving me the opportunity I needed. I kicked at her bad knee and sent her tumbling to the ground, flat on her back. She still held the prod in her outstretched hand, and, when its point dropped into a puddle, her entire body convulsed from the brief shock.

My stomach turned at what I had to do. I grabbed the knife and pulled, clenching my teeth so Ma couldn't hear me scream. When I pulled the knife free, I was on the verge of fainting. Somehow, though, I had enough presence of mind to apply pressure to the wound.

She was back on her feet and smiled darkly. "You're stronger than you look. Maybe if Daisy knew that, she might have stuck around. Told me you were a wimp."

She swung the prod at me like a sword, and I deflected the first pass with the knife.

"She did stick around! She n-n-never would have left."

Though she was breathing a little heavier now, Ma snickered. "You think so? Rachel or no Rachel, Daisy was going to take off the minute she got the chance. I heard her say so."

I launched forward with the knife, and Ma side-stepped me. Because of my leg injury, I was much slower now, and she had the advantage. "What the hell are you talking about?"

That's when she told me what happened the day I left. Daisy came into the kitchen and asked to use the phone to call her ex. She apologized to him for running away and begged him to take her back. She told him she was having his baby, and she wanted them to be a family.

"They talked for hours," Ma said. "While you were off buying her 'engagement ring,' she was making plans to leave you." Ma swung her head back and gave a belly laugh. "You were never more than a meal ticket to that girl, a way to support that baby you ended up killing."

"You're lying!" I snarled and lunged for her exposed throat.

She dodged me and stuck out a foot that sent me flying through the air and crashing on my wounded leg. "Why would I?" she asked. "I might have told a couple of fibs to keep you here, but what do I care now?"

My physical and emotional stress had worn me down to the point that I almost believed her. "That can't be true," I protested, and my voice broke as I choked back tears.

"I bet you got a busy signal when you called," she chuckled. "It was your fiancée blabbing on the phone with her baby daddy. Land sakes, you're stupid!"

Ma underestimated me. She thought that taunting me like that would break me, but she forgot that her previous snide jokes had always sent me into a blind rage. I was no longer heartbroken. I was infuriated by the way Ma, Daisy, and Rachel had manipulated me. With the other two dead, I could only lash out at Ma.

My roar was so menacing even Ma was scared, and that's when I charged. She ducked as I arched the knife up, and I sliced off a piece of her scalp.

Her flesh whirled through the air and plopped into the pond, where it was gulped down by a passing turtle. She grasped at her head and howled as blood trickled down her face.

Whether she bled out or lived to torture another hiker, I no longer cared. Since she was temporarily disabled, I had time to escape, so I grabbed her prod and sprinted back to the fence. It was now or never. I was out of choices and needed to use Red's body to short out the fence. I lifted it up with a bear hug.

"Sorry, friend," I whispered, throwing him against the fence. I jumped back and turned away. If it was going to be anything like Tornado's electrocution, I didn't want to watch.

But nothing happened. I waited a little longer, and when I turned around, Red's body was still slumped against the chain links.

"What were you expecting?" Ma asked. She was still clutching her head, but she smiled. "Fireworks?"

I laughed. "I can't believe you were dumb enough not to turn the fence back on after I turned it off. You even showed me how to use the switch. I pegged you for someone smarter than that."

Ma was unfazed. "Oh, you think so? Boy, you are so dumb. The big switch works the bathroom light. This fence was never on to begin with. Do you have any idea how much it would cost to keep that sucker running all day and night? Who could afford that? Besides, I can't imagine what the neighbors would think." She slapped her knee in glee. "You could have climbed it any time!"

"Then what about Tornado?"

"Oh, I only switch it on when I need to."

"And I know the fence was on when Peter was driving us out."

Ma sniffed. "The last time he accidentally let someone escape, I had a devil of a time tracking the hiker down and bringing her back. I didn't want to take any chances this time."

"Well, what matters now is that the power's off, and I'm out of here." I held out the cattle prod. "Come any closer and I'll zap the hell out of you."

With a last-minute jitter in my heart, I scrambled over to Red's body. Standing on his shoulders gave me the extra height I needed to start the climb up, but each step was agony when my bare toes pressed into the metal of the chain links. I had to rely more on what little upper body strength I could muster to pull myself the rest of the way to the top.

When I got there, I dropped my head and arms over the rail and hung a few moments, relieved to be finished with the toughest part. I figured if I stayed there another minute or so and regained my strength, I could pull the rest of my body up and over.

I turned to the nightmare I was leaving behind. Red and Rachel's bodies were both still in clear view, and they reminded me of the other dead hikers. My hands and clothes were covered in blood, and I realized it was impossible to tell which stain belonged to whom. Some of them were Daisy's. Some could be Ma's, too. Even she was bleeding.

I had only been in this hell for three days, but it felt like an eternity. Before it all happened, I started out an ordinary guy from Illinois, and now I was surrounded by murderers and thieves. I couldn't wait to be away from the farm and everyone I'd met along the way.

The first thing I'm going to do is take a long shower. Then maybe I'll hire a shrink; though, I'm sure that would do much good, because I can't imagine opening up about what really happened.

But it didn't matter what I'd do when I got to the other side. At least I'd be safe. That was when I saw Sparky appear.

"Hurry up, Sparky! The power is off! Grab my hand, and I'll pull you up!" He kept walking toward Ma, as though he hadn't heard, a dirty flour sack dangling from one hand. The tops of the chain links were digging deep into my armpits, and I knew I couldn't tolerate the pain much longer.

"Come on, Sparky! Don't be stupid. We can both get out of here, but you've got to hurry! I can't hold on much longer."

When he didn't answer again, I swung a leg over and straddled the top. "Suit yourself."

I couldn't resist a parting shot at Ma. "Screw you!"

"Ooh, that hurts!"

"Admit it, Ma. I beat you!"

"Winner, winner, chicken dinner!" She gave me the finger and turned to Sparky. "I've had enough."

I was about to swing the rest of my body over the top and drop to the ground when Sparky yelled. "Wait!"

I should never have hesitated. The last thing I saw was him aiming a small remote-control device at the fence.

Sparks flew and Strider convulsed, as massive current shot through his body. His eyeballs popped out and his skin steamed as his hands clamped on the top rail. When his fingers opened again his limp body crumbled to the ground on the other side. A few bones poked out of his skin when he landed.

"He made it!" Sparky applauded.

"No, he didn't. Doesn't count if they're dead before they hit the ground."

Sparky whined, "Why'd you let him talk so long, Ma? Now I have to walk all the way around to pick him up."

"Quit your yapping and use the side gate." She gestured to a small swinging metal gate about twenty feet from where they stood.

He slapped a hand to his forehead. "Oh, duh. Why didn't I think of that?"

"I don't know," she laughed. "Why didn't they? And turn off the juice, will you? That thing costs real money."

He pushed the button again to shut off the electricity and scurried out the tiny door with his wheelbarrow.

"What do you think, Sparky? Did it take him longer to die than the other ones?"

He scratched his chin. "Longer than Tornado, but not as long as that guy last year."

Ma let out a giggle. "Land sakes, how could I forget him? It was quite a show. He was bigger than the redhead."

Sparky rolled Strider's body over to Ma for inspection.

"Perfect," she said. "Let's bury him beside Daisy. That way those two love birds can be together forever. I always like a happy ending, don't you? And I think you can wait to fish that psycho's body out of the pond until tomorrow. She'll keep another day. Just promise to do it before I take my afternoon swim. Meet you in the garden." *Beep, beep.* She backed up her golf cart and headed off.

He threw Red's corpse on top of Strider's and pushed the wheelbarrow toward the garden, where Ma was looking up at the oncoming storm. "Timing's just right for planting," she said, making a beeline for the house for some seeds.

As the first drops fell, Sparky layered the corpses with compost, and finished by placing painted signs on the graves. Sparky crossed out "Rachel," with a permanent marker, replacing it with "Red."

"All done. Red's Radicchio," he said excitedly.

Ma rolled her eyes. "You aren't done yet, and you know it. What's this I hear about two bodies in a cabin? Why aren't they in plots yet?"

Sparky blushed. "I'm sorry, Mom, I got so busy, I forgot. And, you know, I did have to bury that big guy twice."

"That's what happens when you don't follow the system." She wagged a finger. "Body and then loose dirt? You were begging for him to get out. I swear, I don't know where your laziness comes from."

Then she gave him a comforting pat on the back. "You did real good with these two. Run along, now. This rain's gonna be a doozy. And don't forget to bring your dog in. Then come up for dinner. I'm making your favorite. Lasagna."

"I can't wait until we can eat that Australian's produce," Sparky said. "I love ethnic food."

He left, but before he got very far, he turned back. "Hey, you know what, Ma? You were right. Digging really is cooler at night."

About the Author

Following an exciting life-long career in advertising, Alan B. Gibson cofounded a video-chat technology startup that often competes for time with his novel writing.

For many years, hikers from the Appalachian Trail worked odd jobs at an apple orchard he and his partner owned in Harpers Ferry, West Virginia. That farm continues to be a source of inspiration for his plots and characters.

If you liked *High Voltage*, please visit my Amazon page to leave a review or check out my other books, *The Dead of Winter* and *Leave No Trace*. For more information about me and my writing, visit www.ABGibson.me. You can also follow me on Facebook, Twitter, and Instagram.